Confessions of
an Accidental
Player

BUSTED

Antony John

flux™
Woodbury, Minnesota

First Edition
First Printing, 2008

Book design by Steffani Sawyer
Cover design by Gavin Dayton Duffy
Cover image © 2008 Onoky/SuperStock

Flux, an imprint of Llewellyn Publications

Library of Congress Cataloging-in-Publication Data
John, Antony.
  Busted : confessions of an accidental player / Antony John.—1st ed.
    p. cm.
  Summary: High school senior Kevin Mopsely tries to remake his image by joining a crowd of popular boys who are known for treating girls badly, but when Kevin's mother, a feminist college professor, comes to campus to teach a course, his strategy backfires badly.
  ISBN 978-0-7387-1373-1
  [1. Interpersonal relations—Fiction. 2. Feminism—Fiction. 3. Popularity—Fiction. 4. Self-perception—Fiction. 5. Self-confidence—Fiction. 6. High schools—Fiction. 7. Schools—Fiction.] I. Title.
  PZ7.J6216Bu 2008
  [Fic]—dc22
                                                           2008017593

Flux
Llewellyn Publications
A Division of Llewellyn Worldwide, Ltd.
2143 Woodale Drive, Dept. 978-0-7387-1373-1
Woodbury, MN 55125-2989, U.S.A.
www.fluxnow.com

Printed in the United States of America

To Pops—the funniest guy I know.

To Gavin—the coolest elevator-button-pushing, drain-inspecting toddler on earth.

To Audrey—simply the best.

1

I'm sorry, but you can't sit there."

A petite redhead hovers beside Abby and me. She looks about twelve, and seems intent on guarding the defenseless cafeteria table against our unwelcome advances.

I'd really like to avoid an argument, so I try to ease Abby away, but she stands her ground defiantly. I'd have more success moving a mountain.

"We're saving that table in case people need it," explains the redhead, smiling sweetly.

Abby mimics her smile. "Well, aren't we lucky, Kevin," she gushes, grabbing my arm. "*We're* people, so it must be ours."

The redhead's smile vanishes and her eyes narrow. I sense the negotiations are not progressing to her satisfaction. "You don't understand," she pouts. "It's for, you know ... *particular* people."

"Oh, we're very particular," Abby assures her.

"But this is—"

"Are you a freshman?"

"What? No *way*! I'm a sophomore."

Abby sighs dramatically and prods me with her index finger. "See? They start indoctrinating them so young these days. This one's a couple of years from puberty, but she already harbors territorial ambitions in the school cafeteria." She pulls me into the chair before I can escape.

Our oppressor's mouth hangs open in shock, but she quickly regains her composure. She cocks one pencil-thin eyebrow, then shoves our table away from hers so it's clear to any passersby that we're not connected. At all. We're an island, Abby and I, a leper colony separated from the social mainland by a few inches that might as well be miles.

"This," huffs Abby, waving her hand around dismissively, "is why we don't eat in the cafeteria."

Which is true. Ever since we got the combination to the large music practice room, we've sequestered ourselves with the other members of our quartet—Abby calls it our pop group, but that's a stretch—and our lunch hours have been significantly less stressful. But today the room is being cleaned.

"Bloody carpet shampooers better be done right quick or I'll give 'em what for," growls Abby, doing a spot-on impersonation of her bubbly British parents.

"If you speak to them in Brit slang, they may not even realize you're pissed."

"After making me eat in the caf, they'll know I'm pissed, all right." She shakes her head and her wavy brown hair falls across her face; she sweeps it behind her ears. "Just look around. It's like they put all the wild animals in one cage as some kind of sick and twisted sociological experiment." She summons a wicked grin, her wide hazel eyes sparkling. "Which begs the question, who's the zookeeper?"

Hiding behind my chicken sandwich, I conduct a quick survey. Not a lot has changed over the past seven months, since the beginning of senior year. The mathletes, stoners, and goths still relegate themselves to the corner tables like they're apologizing for their existence. Which leaves the center tables for the more aesthetically pleasing groups like jocks (who eat loudly) and cheerleaders (who talk loudly about eating).

"There is no zookeeper," I conclude. "He's too afraid of the animals to come anywhere near here."

Abby smacks my arm playfully. "Who said the zookeeper was a guy?"

I roll my eyes, but I can't help chuckling. Abby's always Abby, even when she's been spurned by a social-climbing sophomore in designer clothing. I wonder what it would be like to be so self-assured.

Abby's comforting patter ceases momentarily as she tucks into her tuna salad sandwich. I check out the center tables again. They seem to be more densely populated than before, like a mosh pit for Brookbank High royalty.

Between nibbles on a lettuce leaf, the redhead leaps up to make space for approaching cheerleaders; she's evidently aware of her place on the food chain. She pulls a table over so it's touching hers, then waves expectantly. It looks as though at least six tables have been joined together, like pieces of a jigsaw puzzle. Clearly the rule about not moving cafeteria furniture doesn't apply to the social elite.

At the center of the jigsaw, with the allure of a rock star and the gravitational pull of an all-star athlete, sits Brandon Trent. He doesn't need to speak loudly, because everyone wants to listen to him. He doesn't need to move around, because everyone comes to him. At the slightest twitch of his chiseled jaw or muscled shoulders, Brandon's loyal followers fall into a swoon. And it's not hard to see why.

When one of the cheerleaders spills ketchup on her impossibly deep scoop-neck sweater, she leans toward Brandon like she can't believe her good fortune. For his part, Brandon already wields a wet paper towel, ready to apply his magic touch to the stain besmirching her chest. He even seems gallant, averting his eyes, but I suspect that his hands are doing the looking for him.

A moment later he magically produces a packet of Cheetos for his right-hand man, Zach Thomas, who responds with a grateful, lobotomized grin. The smattering of sarcastic applause that ensues successfully identifies Brandon as unquestioned leader and Zach as erstwhile goon.

Brandon's batting two-for-two, and now there's the expectation of further miracles. Everyone is holding their breath, awaiting ever more impressive feats of empathy, dexterity, and general heroism. He may be effortlessly charismatic, but there are times that Brookbank High's obsession with Brandon Trent seems slightly bizarre and borderline pathological.

"He's a jerk," snorts Abby. "Now stop eavesdropping."

"What do you mean? I wasn't—"

"Kevin," she says sternly. "I can see you watching Brandon. Let's focus. Did you get new pads put on your flute keys yet?"

"Affirmative, captain."

Abby's nose crinkles as she laughs. She's still got tuna in her mouth. "So we're set for practice tomorrow."

"Also affirmative."

"What about 'captain'? I liked that."

"Also affirmative, *captain*," I reply obediently.

Abby bows her head gracefully, like a character from a Jane Austen novel. "Thank you, trusty manservant," she says in perfect Queen's English, then resumes eating. I notice there's no lettuce in her sandwich.

"Hold on. How come you're the captain and I'm the servant?"

"Because I play the double bass and you play the flute. You may be the best musician in the city, but you still play the ... well, the *flute*."

"It's not my fault Mom had a flute lying around at home."

"I know, Kevin. I know." She pats my arm sympathetically.

"Anyway, if we could just do an arrangement of 'California Dreamin',' you'd hear how cool a flute solo can sound."

Abby groans. "We're not doing songs by the Mamas and the Papas. No one even knows who they are."

"But it's the best flute solo in the entire history of pop music."

"And there are so many to choose from!"

I narrow my eyes and pretend to sulk, so Abby drapes her arm comfortingly across my shoulders. It feels good, and makes me wonder what it must be like to be Brandon, whose broad shoulders are rarely seen without a slender female arm as an accessory. I feel my eyes dragged back to him magnetically. I tune in to his conversation.

"Her name's Tiffany," Brandon explains, wielding a photograph for admiring onlookers. "She's a junior at Brookbank University ... Dean's List, captain of the varsity gymnastics team, and her dad's VP of McGuffin Industries."

Everyone at the table "whoas" and "dudes" approvingly, although I'd be amazed if they know what a VP is. Or Dean's List, come to think of it. Truth is, not many of Brandon's friends aspire to academic excellence.

"I think Tiffany wants to take our relationship to the next level," continues Brandon, nodding in agreement with himself. "Yesterday we were driving around in my mom's Lexus, rehashing that old 'Was Freud a misogynist?' debate, when she leans over and places her hand firmly on my—"

The bell splits the air and lunch is over. Everyone at his extended table exchanges the kind of glances that say, *are we really going to stop here*? I figure Brandon must be pissed he didn't get to finish his story, but actually he's the first to get up. The other guys jostle for the right to be next in line.

"I guess we should go," says Abby.

"Uh-huh."

As he saunters through the cafeteria with his posse in tow, Brandon runs a hand absently through his sun-bleached hair. Girls swoon and the kitchen staff smiles and teachers wave. Before they've even made it to the door, Brandon and his merry men have been surrounded by the most beautiful girls from the senior class. Taylor Carson, class president and aspiring thespian, casts a smoldering gaze, but Brandon just walks by; Morgan Giddes, cheerleading captain, and Paige Tramell, homecoming queen, sidle up like twin contestants for *America's Next Top Model* and bite their lower lips provocatively, but Brandon pretends not to notice. The guy has ice in his veins.

I look at the table just vacated by the posse. They forgot to clear their plates, but already an elderly member of the kitchen staff has trundled out. She cleans Brandon's place first.

"Are you coming or not?" Abby stands over me, drumming her fingers against her arm. "The bell rang fifty seconds ago."

"Oh, yeah." I jump up, much to her amusement, and she links our arms as we leave.

"Hey, wait," she says. "You didn't eat your sandwich."

Oops. I'd completely forgotten about the sandwich. "I'm not hungry," I lie.

"I understand. This place is like kryptonite for your appetite. Hold a hot dog eating contest here and the contestants would be heaving in seconds."

I snort loudly and the sound resonates around the mostly empty cafeteria. At the doorway, Paige Tramell glances over her shoulder, seeking out the source of this unsavory disturbance. Fleetingly we make eye contact, and as she exits, her beautiful face and stunning figure remain branded on my memory. My heart flutters wildly.

When I calm down I realize that Abby is dragging me out, her fingers twined with mine.

She's holding my hand.

And I hadn't even noticed.

2

"All right, everyone, let's have some quiet."

Ms. Kowalski sounds tired, or bored, or possibly both, which is how she always sounds first thing in the morning. Her monotone is several decibels too low for a high school teacher, so roll call is a prolonged undertaking.

"Mopsely."

I grunt manfully in my best imitation of Brandon, but it just sounds like I'm shifting phlegm around in my throat.

"D'ya need the Heimlich?" Abby stage whispers. She grins contentedly, knowing it's way too early in the day for me to summon a witty retort.

Ms. K concludes roll call and sighs. "I believe that Brandon has an announcement," she says without enthusiasm.

Brandon doesn't speak for a while, but he knows we won't interrupt. Eventually he leans forward and feigns seriousness. "Graduation Rituals," he says sharply. "Lunchtime. Here."

His posse whoops and stamps their feet beneath the tables as Ms. Kowalski struggles unsuccessfully to restore order. Brandon affords them a moment to express their adulation, then raises his open palms as a call for silence; unlike Ms. Kowalski, he is met with utter compliance.

"Yes, well, you may complete your announcement now," says Ms. K breathlessly.

Brandon smiles warmly and shakes his head. "Now, now, Ms. Kowalski. I think we both know there's nothing to add. Everybody knows about the Graduation Rituals."

This pronouncement induces more cheering from the posse and more futile arm flailing from Ms. K, who seems genuinely relieved when the bell rings and homeroom ends. School has barely begun, but she's already leaning against her desk like a drooping leaf.

Brandon's cronies pull out their cell phones and begin texting in unison. I peer over and notice that they're forwarding his announcement to the rest of the senior class, like the Graduation Rituals are major news. Predictably, I've never heard of them.

On his way out, Brandon schmoozes like a seasoned pro. He compliments Morgan's makeup and she coos. He applauds Paige's revealing outfit and she beams. When Taylor asks if she can run her fingers over his new calfskin messenger bag, he obliges her with a broad smile. Even the ugliest of his loyal henchmen are greeted with hugs and kisses, accruing status points simply by trailing in his wake.

I look at my own book bag—a camouflaged Eddie Bauer

special edition that Brandon popularized at the beginning of freshman year. Now mine is the only one in school, and I'm not entirely sure that's a good thing. At least, I don't recall Taylor ever asking to run her hand over my bag's 100 percent nylon.

Brandon's almost out the door when he signals for the entourage to back up. "Ms. Kowalski," he exclaims, "I almost forgot to tell you how much I'm enjoying homeroom these days. I love that you keep things so relaxed, you know?"

"Oh." Ms. K studies her hands as her mouth twitches involuntarily into a smile. "Thank you."

"No, Ms. Kowalski. Thank *you*," he insists, striding toward her and patting her arm gently.

She keeps her eyes averted as he turns away, and doesn't see his bag swinging around. It knocks her against the whiteboard. When she collects herself, I notice that the diagrammed sentences from yesterday's lessons have been transferred to her blouse.

I step forward. "Ms. Kow—"

"No, don't," Abby whispers. "What's she going to do about it? I doubt she brings a spare blouse to work."

"But the writing—"

"Might come out, or it might not. But letting her know it's there is just going to make her feel self-conscious." She clenches her fist. "Brandon's such a jerk."

"What? No way. It was an accident."

"Sure. Everything's an accident with Brandon."

"What's that supposed to mean?"

Abby shakes her head. "It's just... everything's a game

to him. He doesn't believe half of what he says. It's all for show."

"That's not true. Everyone likes Brandon."

"Sure they do. He's the most popular guy in school, but even that's a game. All he cares about is winning the popularity contest." She slings her bag onto her back angrily. "I guess the ends justify the means."

"What are you talking about?"

She sighs, turns away. "Nothing. Just forget it."

I really want to know what's gotten into her, but Abby's icy demeanor deters me. Intimidation is one of her gifts.

As we shuffle between the tables I glance at Ms. Kowalski's blouse again, wondering how long it will take her to get the stain out. It's a shame really, because the blouse looked new, like a gift to herself for making it through yet another school year. Maybe it was a way of bribing herself to keep working, even though she's tired of her job. My dad did the same thing eight months ago—hated his job so much that he went out and got himself something new to make life seem interesting again. I'm glad for Ms. K that she settled on a blouse.

"Kevin, can I have a word?"

Ms. K beckons me away from the door as if she's afraid my classmates might be lurking outside, eavesdropping. She needn't worry—eavesdropping implies a level of celebrity I'll never achieve.

Abby waggles her finger at me as she heads off to class. "I told you they'd find out you did it."

"Find out you did *what?*" asks Ms. K, concerned.

"Nothing. Abby's just teasing me."

"Oh. That's quite funny."

"Yes. And I'm her favorite target."

"Indeed." For a moment, Ms. K's eyebrows rise inquiringly, but then she clears her throat. "Kevin, I, um, just wondered if your mom is still teaching at Brookbank University?"

"Yes."

"Good, good."

"Why are you asking?"

"Hmmm? Oh, I just wondered." She waves my question away with a flick of her hand and an open smile. "I trust that *you* won't be going to Brandon's meeting?"

Her question catches me off guard. Ever since parent-teacher night my freshman year she's taken a personal interest in my studies, but never in my extracurricular activities. I'm about to say no, they'd probably kill me if I showed up, but then I realize what she's really saying is that even the teachers know I'm not cool enough to belong to Brandon's group.

Over the past four years I've become reconciled to belonging to what Abby calls a "select minority," but hearing a teacher acknowledge my unpopularity marks a new low. I want to tell her she's wrong, only I'm pretty sure she's not, so instead I hover moodily while she tucks her hair behind her ears. But then I remember that the bell rang three minutes ago, so I take off—because I hate being late.

Which I guess is incontrovertible proof that Ms. K has me pegged.

3

It wasn't always like this. There was a time when my progress toward Acceptable Boyfriend Material seemed steady, if unspectacular.

The first breakthrough occurred in spring of fifth grade. During the annual hobbies class I performed a flute piece called "Dance of the Blessed Spirits," by the unfortunately named Christoph Willibald von Gluck. It's one of those great pieces that make you sound like a virtuoso, even though it's the pianist who's really doing all the work.

My accompanist was sweating profusely by the end, but I remained a model of calm professionalism. And I would have stayed that way if Natasha Williams and her butt-length black hair hadn't padded over and praised me on every aspect of my performance. She even asked if she could touch my flute, which seemed like an innocent enough request. After

I made her apply antibacterial gel to both hands, I handed it over.

I'll never forget the look on her face: reverential, inspired. Her eyes flitted from me to my flute, like she was seeing me for the first time. I was only ten, but the electricity between us was palpable. I knew that things would never be the same.

Natasha took about ten deep breaths, shifting her weight from one leg to the other.

"Would you be willing to, like, you know, give me flute lessons?" she asked finally. "That was such a nice piece you played. I'd like to be able to do that. Will you give me lessons? Please?"

She spoke so falteringly that I could tell she was nervous. Normally I'd have been nervous too, but we were talking about the flute, of all things. This was my turf. I felt emboldened.

"Natasha, have you got a crush on me?" I teased.

Natasha froze. Her face flashed pink, then red, then a deep burgundy that didn't seem entirely human. I began to suspect that her next words might not be as complimentary as I'd initially hoped.

"Kevin Mopsely, you...you *butthole*," she snapped, clattering the flute on the desk. "Just forget it, okay?"

As she stormed out of the room, I couldn't help wondering why I hadn't just said "yes"; a few weekly lessons is all she'd have needed to realize that my dorky reputation wasn't entirely justified. And then we'd probably have started dating, I'm sure of it. After all, she never actually denied having a crush on me.

But it was not to be. Instead, I was absolutely right in supposing that things would never be the same between us. That was the last time Natasha ever spoke to me.

4

Perhaps it was inevitable . . . after blowing such a gift-wrapped opportunity, I was bound to suffer what might be termed a "girl drought"; I just hadn't counted on the drought lasting four years. But it was fall of ninth grade before my flute and I again attracted attention from the opposite sex. And even then it was Alyssa Gregoire, whose goofy-cute combination was amply offset by her questionable personal hygiene.

I should have realized straight away that Alyssa and I were not destined to be together. Her idea of social climbing was a fervent desire to join the Band Geeks, the musicians' clique of which I was unofficial head and, technically, one third of the membership. (Ben Walton, our fourth member, had just left by mutual agreement after he failed my weekly pop quiz on music theory.) I was proud to be a Band Geek, but even I was aware that we were pretty low on the social totem pole.

Besides, I had other reasons to question Alyssa's sudden interest in the Band Geeks. She had recently begun announcing that she aspired to be the best flutist in school, which meant supplanting me. So it seemed only natural to question whether she was joining my clique, or infiltrating it.

Then, one lunchtime, she plopped down at our table and asked to try out my flute. I figured she meant she just wanted to touch it, but she pieced it together and started blowing. Her embouchure was all messed up because she'd just gotten braces, and spit flew everywhere. But she still gushed about the lightness of the key mechanism, and said how jealous she was that I had a solid silver flute while hers only had a silver mouthpiece. She said it nicely, too, with a gentle singsong voice and a lopsided smile that emphasized her cuteness and made me momentarily forget her odor.

She continued talking, but I wasn't really listening. I had already put my lips on the flute, absently fingering the opening notes of a Handel sonata while thinking about the way our saliva was being commingled on the silver mouthpiece. It was like French kissing, except without the danger of injury from her braces. And even though we were only sharing a fake Frenchie, it was still an incredible turn-on. So much so that I didn't hear her until she started shouting.

"Kevin, why are you moaning?"

I froze. "Was I?"

"Yeah!" She continued shouting, like her volume control had gotten stuck on High.

I looked around the cafeteria. Everyone had stopped to watch.

"Sorry," I whispered.

She hesitated. "Did you clean my spit off first?" Another pause. "You did clean my spit off first, didn't you?" A long pause—the horror of dawning recognition. "Omigod, you're sharing my saliva! You're sharing my saliva and . . . and *moaning!*"

Moments later, I'd not only been deposed as head of the Band Geek clique, but kicked out of it as well. While she munched contentedly at the dirt beneath her finger nails, Alyssa assured my former clique-mates that she'd assume my leadership responsibilities. It was undoubtedly the low point of my life.

I didn't play my flute again at school for the rest of the year, which meant that Alyssa had achieved her objective of becoming the school's best flutist. And it only took her five minutes.

I probably would have kept my flute playing entirely private if I hadn't found The Picture while I was rummaging through Mom and Dad's closets the summer before tenth grade. It was just a photo on the cover of an ancient LP, but it changed everything: Herbie Mann, funky guy with a funky name, standing stark naked except for a flute draped provocatively across his shoulders. His album was called *Push, Push*, which seemed pretty suggestive too. Oh, and the LP occupied a primo spot in Mom's most secret drawer, right on top of her copy of *The Joy of Sex*. True, the book was still wrapped in cellophane and hidden in a drawer—which didn't seem like an auspicious sign for my parents' sex lives—but the symbolism was obvious. Back in 1971, naked male flute players were sex symbols—the Justin Timberlakes of their day. Maybe Herbie Mann himself was Justin Timberlake's inspiration. It was such a groundbreaking moment that I didn't even feel particularly guilty about invading my parents' privacy.

I was certain this was a sign that things would be different in high school. Weren't teachers always telling me that fashion is cyclical, that if you wait a while everything becomes cool again? I'd be the Herbie Mann of Brookbank High—nothing but me, my flute, and a parade of hot girls.

But two days later something happened to turn all that on its head: Abby and her parents moved in next door.

I remember watching Abby lugging heavy furniture into the house while the movers sat around complimenting her parents on their fine tea. When she needed a break, Abby dragged out her double bass and began playing, right there in the middle of the yard. Passersby gawked at her, but she either didn't notice or didn't care. She was imperious, a force of nature, and I wondered what it would feel like to have that sort of courage, that self-belief.

I opened my window a crack and started playing the flute, hoping she'd notice. Thirty seconds later there was thunderous banging at the front door. I rushed downstairs to open it and Abby stood before me, all bushy hair and serious, straight eyebrows.

"Finding duets for *this* ensemble is going to be a real nightmare," she announced, like she was warning me of rough seas ahead.

"I'll do an arrangement," I blurted, momentarily forgetting to be cool.

"It's a deal then." She stretched out her hand. "I'm Abby, by the way."

"Um, K-Kevin," I said smoothly.

"Great. Well, I'll come back around dinnertime. Our place is a wreck right now. Oh, and I eat anything, so if you've got leftovers…"

She clomped back to the moving van and clambered inside. Moments later she staggered out, an impossibly large antique bureau clasped awkwardly between her arms. I ought to have offered to help, but I couldn't. I just stood there, watching her, overcome by a mixture of amazement and envy.

That was the beginning of Abby and me: the Inseparable Duo.

She showed up that evening, just as she'd said she would. She ate Mom's food like it was the finest she'd ever tasted, and the two of them chatted like long-lost best buddies. I began to wonder if I should just sneak off and leave them to it.

After dinner, Abby carried her bass into the living room and we played through my arrangement of "Ob-La-Di, Ob-La-Da" by the Beatles, which I'd picked because it has a simple but prominent bassline; she played it like it was the easiest thing in the world, but her smile told me she was enjoying herself anyway. Next, I pulled out an arrangement of Van Morrison's "Moondance," with a significantly jazzier bassline and a flashier flute solo; it sounded surprisingly good, although I couldn't help thinking what a difference adding piano and drums would make.

When we paused for a drink, Abby picked up my flute.

"Do you mind if I try playing it?" she asked.

"Go for it."

While she tried to hone the breathy sound emerging from my flute, I focused on banishing my memories of Natasha and Alyssa.

A minute later she handed the flute back to me in defeat. "Your keys have got holes in them," she huffed.

"It's an open-holed flute. Produces a better tone, plus it also forces you to master your fingering technique."

She peered up at me from under her dark eyebrows. "Did you, um, just say you're an expert at *fingering*?"

I recognized that all-too-familiar look of shock; it was happening all over again. My brain jerked into flashback mode, replaying classic footage from my Natasha and Alyssa nightmares.

"N-No, no, no. Not like that. I mean ... not that sort of fingering."

Abby cracked up. "I'm just teasing, Kevin. But you have to admit, complimenting yourself on your fingering is pretty bold when we've only known each other an hour."

"Well, yeah. But I didn't exactly mean it like—"

"Kidding again, Kevin!" Abby coiled a strand of hair around her finger, then tucked it behind her ear. "I'm sorry. I know I shouldn't do that, but I just can't help it." She shrugged. "Oh, whatever. You'll get used to it pretty quick."

I felt a wave of relief and anticipation. "So, you'll come over again?"

"You betcha. Your Mom's cooking is amazing."

"Oh." I tried not to look too disappointed that my mom's food was more enticing than my company.

"Kidding again, Kevin," groaned Abby. "It's you I want to come hang out with, not your mom ... Wow, I'm really gonna have to work on you, huh?"

"'Fraid so," I said. But secretly I couldn't wait for the work to start.

Things haven't changed significantly over the past few years. We're best friends, confidants, and partners in crime, but that's all. Contrary to popular belief, we're not, nor have we ever been, an item—although Abby's constant presence ensures that no other girl will look twice at me. It's like she forms an exclusion zone for unidentified estrogen.

Not that we don't have fun together, but sometimes I feel like we resemble a comedy duo instead of a potential couple. We have the kind of Laurel and Hardy relationship that makes Ms. Kowalski laugh at my expense, the kind of chemistry that makes me seem not just uncool, but borderline asexual. We're friends without benefits, Abby and me. And there's a reason they call them benefits.

I've had eighteen years to be noticed, to be *somebody*, but so far all I've accomplished is a near miss with Natasha, a fake Frenchie with Alyssa, and an eternally platonic coupling with Abby. I am what I've always been: official class dork, ignored by anyone remotely popular. Even when including teachers, I can count my friends on one hand. So I guess that Ms. Kowalski is right about me. Maybe she knows me even better than I know myself.

But that's about to change. There's less than two months of high school remaining. It's time I made them count.

"Dude. Like. Whoa."

Spud Beasley has a way with words, so everyone maintains a respectful silence until they're sure he's finished. Even then they all wait until it's absolutely, positively clear he's satisfied with his little pearl of wisdom.

Got to hand it to Spud—he may speak with the directness of one of his infamous curveball pitches, but he always has an audience. Of course, the reason he has an audience is because he's like that dwarf Gimli in the *Lord of the Rings* movies: all grunts and simmering testosterone. If we were ever crazy enough to give him an ax, he'd probably take out half the school before anyone even noticed he'd gone postal in the first place. Rumor is, his latest counselor describes him as "volatile."

No one knows what happened to the other counselors.

"Dude. Like … Whoa."

Spud's done it again, which is really interfering with Brandon's account of yesterday evening's dalliance with Tiffany. I get the feeling Brandon would like to ask Spud to keep his guttural sounds to himself, but he's aware that college juniors won't be so attracted to him if he's missing a limb or two.

Instead, he waits for Spud.

Everyone waits for Spud.

Spud nods to show he's finished.

Everyone breathes again.

Brandon looks at his watch. "What the hell, let's get started."

He ambles to the front of the classroom, apparently pleased with the turnout for the meeting: a full quota of guys from the baseball, football, and basketball teams, plus other aspiring alpha males. As he opens his arms wide in a gesture of welcome, his smile morphs into a smirk, and before I can catch up with what's happening, he's cackling demonically and his infectious laugh has everyone in the room laughing with him. I join in too, although it's tough to feign laughter when you're petrified. I feel a sense of masochistic pride just for having the nerve to be here.

Brandon looks around the room, sizing us up. Zach, his brown-nosing protégé, stamps the ground excitedly when Brandon looks over at him, but Brandon just flips him the bird and keeps on scanning. Eventually he sees me.

"What the f—"

I shift my butt on the plastic chair and conjure a nervous smile. I don't belong here, and I've already been found out. Thank God he didn't actually use the f-word.

"Mopsely, what the fuck are you doing here?"

Oh well, at least he knows my name.

I take a deep breath. "I just, um, want to be part of the, the... you know, the Graduation, er..." Crap. I can't remember the name. *I can't even remember the name.* "A part of the, er..."

"The Graduation Rituals," says Brandon, as if this is becoming too painful even for him.

"Yeah, the Rituals."

Brandon's smirk is back and everyone is pretending to try not to laugh, so the laughter comes out in coughs and snorts. I can feel my face flashing red, heating the air around me.

"Right," says Brandon gravely. "So, which part of the Graduation Rituals were you hoping to be involved in? Maybe the Alternative Yearbook, huh?" Everyone laughs. "Or maybe the Strategic Graffiti Campaign?" Everyone laughs even louder. "No, no, I know... you want to compile the Book of Busts, right? That must be it. Come on, Mopsely, tell us which one. You just say what you want and it's yours."

I know he's not serious, and so does everyone else—their laughter is so riotous that I want to evaporate. Two minutes in and all I can think about is getting away. But as the noise dies down Brandon's still staring at me, like he's actually waiting for me to respond. Somehow the silence is even worse than laughter.

Okay, Kevin, think. What were the options again? Something about graffiti (oh God, no), and... and... I'm about to ask Brandon to repeat the list when I remember the Book of Busts. Now, that I can handle. After all, tons of people have been busted—big time—at Brookbank High this year. Like that freshman who got an essay published in Seventeen magazine before they realized it was plagiarized. Or the two juniors who got caught trying to shoplift a pair of Manolo Blahniks, then threatened to sue the store when they discovered they were knockoffs. Or the guy who broke his thermometer in chem lab just to get the school evacuated while the hazmat team cleared up the mercury.

"Yo, Earth to Mopsely. What's it going to be?" yawns Brandon.

I swallow hard. "Um, maybe the Book of Busts."

More laughter.

"Get real, Mopsely," explodes Zach. "Like Brandon's gonna let you anywhere near the Book of Busts!"

Brandon looks up sharply. He doesn't seem to appreciate the interruption. "Why shouldn't I, Zach?"

"Because I'm compiling the book. Remember? It's mine."

"I think that's up to me. Or are you in charge now?"

Zach blanches. "But Kevin's a dork. He probably doesn't even know what the Book of Busts is."

"Or maybe he's not a dork," counters Brandon, like he's forgotten I'm sitting two feet away from him. "And maybe he *does* know about the book."

"Bullshit."

Suddenly, there's total silence. Brandon remains completely, eerily still, staring at Zach unblinkingly. I feel caught in the middle of a battle of wills, and neither side appears to be backing down.

Brandon takes a deep breath and claps a hand on my

shoulder. "The Book of Busts is a *calling*, Mopsely. Do you get what I'm saying?" I nod, although I truly have no idea what he's talking about. "Generations of Brookbank seniors have compiled the book. It's a serious business. Zach doesn't think you're up to it. What do *you* think?"

I can feel every pair of eyes boring into me. They all know I'm a fraud. I know I'm a fraud. Now I just want to get out of this unscathed.

"S-Sure, Brandon. I'm up to it."

Brandon narrows his eyes and leans over the table. "Yeah? Zach doesn't think so. So how about you tell him where you plan to start?"

I know this is make-or-break time. Either I say something smart and get to walk away with my dignity, or I fail miserably and enter the FBI Witness Protection Program.

"I, er . . . " I stall for time, mentally filing through Brookbank's catalog of busts. And then it hits me: "I'd start with Taz Green and Erica Roberts," I blurt out. "I mean, that's got to be the biggest bust."

There's a moment's pause, but suddenly Brandon is smiling and smacking me on the back playfully. And then most of the rest of the guys start laughing and whooping too.

"Shit," Brandon exclaims, like it's the ultimate compliment. "I have to admit it, Mopsely, you're dead on . . . that is the biggest bust, probably in school history. What do you say now, Zach? You still think Kev's a dork?"

Zach curls his upper lip and flashes a tortured smile, his bright white teeth like a neat row of tombstones.

I can't help thinking that Taz and Erica's breakup is probably *not* the biggest bust in school history. But as it involved some suspect pot and an inflatable doll, it certainly scores high on shock value. In any case, I'm too relieved to disagree.

"So, Mopsely...I mean, Kev," continues Brandon earnestly, "I want you to know we're all here for you, okay? Like you say, you're going to want to start with Taz, 'cause he's the only one who dated Erica. I reckon he'll be more than willing to spill the beans—"

I'm nodding furiously, but after the way Taz got caught, I figure he'll be the last person to talk.

"—And then you'll need to talk to all the guys here, see what they can come up with for you, you know?" Brandon pauses, so I automatically nod. "But there'll still be gaps, and you're really going to have to use some ingenuity." Another pause. Another nod. "What I'm saying is, it's a lot of work. We'll be meeting every week—twice a week if we have to— so you've got be committed. You are committed, right?"

I gaze longingly at the door. "Um, yeah."

Brandon stares Zach down triumphantly, then smacks my back again. "Wow, and to think, all this time I thought you were a total loser." He sweeps his arm across his body as though preaching to everyone present. "But you've shown us we need to be open-minded...Turns out, not every guy who plays the flute is a complete fag."

It's as close to a compliment as I've ever heard from Brandon, and even though I feel like I've just been adopted as the group's geeky mascot, I can't suppress a smile. I'm going get through this after all.

Now all the guys except Zach are cheering and stamping again, and with my fears temporarily assuaged, I bob my head in time with their rhythmic clapping. The room hums with energy as Brandon reaches into his bag and presents me with a folder emblazoned with the words "Book of Busts."

"For the record," he whispers conspiratorially, confident that everyone is listening, "I'll take care of Morgan Giddes. Word is, the chick's a virgin, so she might need some special attention."

While Brandon silences the applause that follows his every announcement, I can't help wondering what happened to Tiffany. But as no one else seems to be concerned with this particular detail, I figure there must be an explanation.

"In the meantime," continues Brandon, "you can start with the measurements of that girl you hang out with … Abby, right? You must have had her a few times by now."

I want to believe I misheard him—but I know I heard him perfectly. My head stops bobbing and I begin hyperventilating. I feel like I'm about to pass out, but since that won't do much for my new reputation, I bury my head in the folder instead.

There's not much inside—just a few pages reproducing the senior portraits of every girl in the class. And below each photo are spaces for her measurements: bust, waist, hips.

Bust, waist, hips.

Bust. Waist. Hips.

Oh crap. *The Book of Busts, in which are recorded the bust, waist, and hip sizes of every senior girl …*

I know I'm burning a peculiar shade of red right now, but I can't help it. My body's wired on adrenaline, my brain's popping like static. One moment I'm calculating the distance to the door in case I decide to make a break for it, the next I'm considering if it's too late to transfer schools. I try to refocus by turning away from the cheering throngs and staring out the window that overlooks the main corridor.

As the guys serenade me with one last round of applause for not being the ignorant dork I actually am, Principal Jefferies passes along the corridor with Ms. Kowalski. Hearing the cheers, they stop to peer through the little window in the door, watching in surprise as I'm welcomed into Brandon's hip fraternity.

Jefferies nods approvingly, in stark contrast to Ms. Kowalski—who shakes her head disappointedly and quickly strides away.

5

As fate would have it, English with Ms. Kowalski is my first class after lunch. I hope that the past ten minutes have been enough time for her to suffer comprehensive short-term amnesia.

Ms. Kowalski stands behind her desk, methodically scanning the class as it settles down like she's weighing each student's worth. It's a study of extremes, that's for sure. In this particular group, the brightest and the stupidest members of the senior class coexist in a state of barely concealed disdain, united only in their utter contempt for me. Which is why it's just as well Ms. K is always on my side. At least, she usually is, but I keep waiting for her to make eye contact with me and she never does. I sense my foray into Brandon's World is about to prove costly to my grade.

"Do you all know about the Graduation Rituals?" she finally asks, fiddling nervously with her bangs.

"Of course," says Morgan Giddes cheerily. "It's where the boys write graffiti in the girls' bathroom stalls, and where the girls get to tell the boys their measurements. Stuff like that."

Most of the class is nodding in agreement, as though this is as obvious and well-known as school being boring and teachers being uncool.

"And how does that make you feel?" continues Ms. K.

"It makes me feel good," shouts Ryan Morton from the back row. "I mean, *real* good—"

"Yes, I'm sure it does, Ryan, but there's really no need to shout in class."

"Was I?" Ryan furrows his unibrow, then studies his lap. "Oh crap, I forgot to turn my iPod down. Sorry."

Ms. K shifts her weight back and forth. I imagine she's wondering if the pleasure of disciplining Ryan is adequate compensation for sacrificing an entire class period; she obviously decides that it's not. "What about you, girls? How do these Graduation Rituals make you feel?"

Paige Tramell raises her hand daintily. "I guess it kind of depends on whether you're pretty and popular. Like, what are they going to write about *me* on the stalls, right? And why would *I* care about revealing photographs?"

Ms. K is getting depressed—I know the signs.

"I mean, like, I'm comfortable with how I look," Paige continues earnestly. "I exfoliate and moisturize twice a day, so I guess I'm going to be okay no matter what kind of photos they take, you know?"

Ms. K blinks slowly, like she's half-expecting that someone as shallow as Paige might not really exist. But when she opens her eyes, Paige is still there, patiently awaiting a response. Ms. K swallows hard. "Doesn't it bother any of you to see women—because that's what you are now—*objectified* like that?"

I look around and quickly work out that no one but me knows what she means. Ms. K has worked it out too.

"What I'm trying to say is, aren't you offended by the idea of judging women only according to their looks?"

Morgan sighs and turns in her seat so that she's addressing the whole class. "I think what Ms. Kowalski is trying to say is, doesn't it upset you all to be misrepresented?"

Ms. K nods enthusiastically. She smiles beatifically at her kindred spirit, and Morgan smiles back, adding, "'Cause I know I'd be pissed as hell if they said I was anything less than a C cup."

Ms. Kowalski is still smiling, but then her face catches up with her brain and she shakes her head violently from side to side.

"No, no, no. You've totally misunderstood me. It's not about cup size, and it shouldn't be about looks, either."

Paige reenters the fray. "Guys, what she's saying is that the whole system's unfair." Ms. K sighs in relief. "Like, it's all fine and dandy for those of us who are cute and popular and all, but what about ugly girls? It must completely suck for them."

Ms. K wrings her hands, but she has evidently given up trying to make her point. In a way, I feel bad for her. She's not even thirty yet, but I can see the idealism that drove her into teaching trickling away every time one of us opens our mouths.

As a last resort, Ms. K glances my way, which is what she does whenever she needs me to explain what she's talking about. But just as quickly, she shakes her head and looks away. I shouldn't be surprised, but I am. I can't help feeling kind of hurt. Because in spite of what she thinks, belonging to Brandon's cohort does not suddenly make me a bad person.

Besides, if the Book of Busts is so offensive, then how come it doesn't bother Paige and Morgan? They seem keen to contribute in any way they can, and I can think of lots of ways they can help me out, both theoretically and practically.

Ms. K shakes her head at me again as I leave the class, but this time I just ignore her.

6

I'm the last to arrive at our quartet rehearsal. Abby's sitting on a stool almost completely hidden by her double bass, and she's practicing a tricky pizzicato passage in the music. It occurs to me that if she'd taken up the cello instead of the bass she might look sexier. She could drape herself over it and wrap her arms around it caressingly.

I cast the image aside as I pull out my flute and fit the pieces together. The rest of the quartet is already set up: Caitlin on drums, Nathan on guitar. Abby bows an A, and Nathan and I tune up while Caitlin pretends to tune her snare drum, which always makes us laugh even though she's been doing it for three years now.

Nathan's latest arrangements are perched on my music stand: some "classic" (i.e., old) pop music; some jazz "standards" (i.e., elevator muzak). It's all kind of corny, but a welcome change from the showpieces I had to learn for last month's instrumental scholarship audition at Brookbank University.

With the slightest nod of my head, I kick-start the first piece. And even though we're sight-reading, the ensemble is tight and the sound crackles with energy. As we draw to a close with a room-rattling crescendo, I can tell from their movements and facial expressions that Abby, Nathan, and Caitlin know we're jamming too. We're sharing *a moment*, and to be honest, it's pretty cool.

An hour later we take a break, and Caitlin and Nathan step outside. They're the ultimate proof that opposites attract. She's waif-like, wears colored contacts, and claims to be the world's first and only Goth-in-red-clothing (because she's allergic to black clothes dye). He's fat, wears thick glasses, and parts his hair carefully to one side; in my less charitable moments I've wondered if he was put on the earth to reassure me that I could be even dorkier than I am. As couples go, Caitlin and Nathan are an enigma, pretty much keeping to themselves whenever we're not rehearsing.

"Where were you at lunch?" Abby asks, laying her double bass gently on its side. "I didn't see you."

I only hesitate for a second. "Finishing some homework. It was due this afternoon."

"Oh." She grabs a couple bottles of water from her book bag and tosses one to me. "That's good to hear. Nathan said you might be at Brandon's meeting, but I figured he must be joking. No way would you join in with that stuff."

I wonder if she knows more than she's letting on, but she takes a big swig and smiles warmly.

"No, of course you wouldn't," she continues. "You're way too cool for them." I honestly think she believes it too.

Nathan and Caitlin are coming back into the room when they pause for a brief kiss. As usual, it morphs into a substantial time-out involving hair pulling and tongues. I can feel myself turning red so I look away, but Abby just laughs.

"Do you think Caitlin would be pleased or offended if I said they're a cute couple?" she whispers.

"I'm not sure 'cute' is the word."

"Of course it is. They're totally in love and they can't get enough of each other. What could be cuter than that?"

"But they look kind of weird together, don't you think?"

Abby picks up her bass. "What's that got to do with whether or not they're a cute couple?"

"I just think of cute couples as being attractive, that's all."

"Like who?" she says, tuning the lowest string.

"Well, like Brandon Trent and Morgan Giddes."

Abby's hands stop moving and she casts me a penetrating stare. "I didn't know they were dating. Who told you that?"

Oh crap. I'm about to tell her they're not dating—at least, not *yet*—but figure that will make things even worse. "It's just an example," I say.

"Well, I don't much like your example. And anyway, what's with your Brandon fetish these days?"

"I do not have a Brandon fetish!"

I pretend to be engrossed in cleaning the spit from my

flute. A moment later Caitlin and Nathan rejoin us, and I escape further interrogation.

We tackle another arrangement and the sound is as crisp as before. But I can't stop dwelling on what Abby just said. What will she think of me when she discovers that I'm hanging out with Brandon? For that matter, what will Brandon and the other guys think when they realize that I'm playing pop song arrangements with some of the least cool people ever to set foot in Brookbank High?

And then it hits me: I just won't tell them. The Book of Busts can be my connection to the coolest guys and girls in school, and the quartet can be the secret hobby that keeps me on good terms with my real friends. Everybody wins.

At the end of the set, Abby pulls out one more arrangement and deposits it silently on our music stands. I glance at the title and do a double take: "California Dreamin'."

"Since this is our last semester together," Abby says, grinning, "I figured it was time we showcased our award-winning flutist."

Nathan and Caitlin cheer. I'm speechless.

"Now, I know you're a perfectionist, Kev," says Abby in a pretend-scolding tone, "but I had to transpose it to a different key so you could play the low notes. The original version was for alto flute."

"I know, I know. Bud Shank played it," I say, still overwhelmed by Abby's gesture. "But he was really an alto saxophonist."

"You mean, an alto sax player took the best flute solo in pop music history?" exclaims Abby in mock outrage.

I ignore her sarcasm. "Yeah. How unfair is that? Like sax

players don't have enough cool solos of their own already." I can almost feel myself reaching for an imaginary soapbox. "And here's another thing, the solo on—"

"Hey, Kevin," Caitlin interrupts, smiling, "you know we share your desire to rid the world of the pernicious and divisive effects of flutophobia, but we've only got fifteen minutes left."

Abby blows me a kiss. "Tell me, is it just coincidence or is there a reason pop flute players have porno names? Herbie Mann, Bud Shank..."

"Kevin Mopsely," chants the usually silent Nathan, like he's trying my name out for size. "Mopsely...the Mopster...the Mopman."

Maybe I should be annoyed, but actually I can't help laughing. In some ways I kind of like it—being a porn star would represent a serious step up from my current state of sexual anonymity.

"Goodness me, Nathan," exclaims Abby. "I hadn't realized that behind that innocent exterior lurks a future *Playboy* editor."

Nathan blushes and smooths down his already flat hair, then starts plucking the opening notes of "California Dreamin'" on his guitar.

Turns out that Abby's arrangement is great: not a note is out of place, not a chord is notated wrongly. Even the flute solo is transcribed perfectly. She must have spent ages doing it.

I play my solo with the same whispery, smoky sound that Bud Shank used on the original recording. When the song's over, Abby decides that we need to play it again, singing the lyrics this time. I look at Nathan, but he just shakes his head.

"You don't mean ... me?" I ask, as my jaw hits the floor.

"Yes!" Abby laughs. "And Caitlin and I will sing the harmonies."

"But I—"

"You'll be great, Kevin. Come on, loosen up."

Nathan is nodding emphatically, so we run it with the lyrics. It's even better than before, and the back-and-forth lines between Abby and Caitlin and me are really tight. By the end of the song I'm on a complete high, and I can see that Abby is too.

"So, guys," she says mischievously, "before you go I have some news. And after today's rehearsal, I think you're going to be pleased to hear it." She runs a hand through her long chestnut hair, which reminds me how pretty she is. "The prom committee has decided to let us perform a live set before the DJ takes over. How cool is that?"

Nathan and Caitlin attempt to high-five, fail miserably, and settle on a moist kiss instead. Abby is bathing in the glory of the moment, and the mood is that of Christmas come early.

I smile too, picturing us together for one last performance. I can already see the mathletes bunched in the corner of the hall, applauding wildly as they identify interesting ratios in the structure of the music. I can imagine the cheerleaders showing off dance moves that have the guys drooling. And then I picture Brandon and his posse ...

Suddenly I'm having trouble maintaining my smile. I try to look as though this is the best news I've had all year, but I'm not sure I'm faking very well. Because in my mind, Brandon's cohort is standing before the stage, mouths agape at the sight of one of their own playing flute in a dorky quartet at our high school prom.

And this is one gig I won't be able to hide.

7

ow was school?" asks Mom.

"Fine," I say, which is what I say most days. I figure that instead of reliving each excruciating detail, I may as well just take the average. *Fine* seems like a reasonable middle ground between the euphoria of quartet practice and the abject humiliation of the Rituals meeting.

"What do you mean by 'fine'?" Mom says, not buying into my rationale.

"You know, everything's normal . . . everything's fine."

"Care to elaborate?"

I think about it. "Not really, no."

Mom sighs emphatically as she pops a gargantuan dish of lasagna into the oven—she seems to have trouble grasping that there are only two of us now. On the floor beside her, Matt the Mutt scurries back and forth doing his finest impression of a robotic vacuum cleaner. When she turns back to me, Mom's wearing her Serious Face.

"Kevin, I feel like we're not communicating well."

"Oh."

She wrings her hands demonstratively. "See? That's just my point. I tell you that I don't think we're communicating well, and you just say 'Oh.' I mean, when the best I can do is elicit a monosyllabic response from my only child, well . . . "

I wait for her to continue, even though I know she's finished. This is one of her rhetorical techniques—stop mid-sentence and allow me to fill in the gap. Apparently it works really well with her students. But I'm just not comfortable relaying today's developments; some things are best left unsaid. Besides, I can guess what has brought on this sudden need for vast quantities of food and a heart-to-heart conversation: she's received an e-mail from Dad, and it has upset her.

And I can imagine why. He's probably pulling his old trick of telling her how much better his life is since he ran off with Kimberly, a fellow realtor who's twelve years younger than Mom. (Apparently he wasn't willing to settle for a Harley like all the other middle-aged guys in town.) And even though I've passed the point of caring, I know it just kills Mom to hear him say it.

"What did he say this time, Mom?"

"I don't know what you're talking about."

"Come on. I thought you wanted us to communicate better."

Mom draws in her breath a couple of times, as if she's

summoning the will to tell me, but then she puts her hand over her mouth and hurries out of the kitchen.

I don't think she's completely over him yet.

As I traipse upstairs to my bedroom, I notice there's a different photo of Dad at the top of the stairs. It must have been taken years ago, because the colors are kind of washed out and he has a full head of hair. He was good-looking back then: rugged, tan, grungy, like he'd just completed a round-the-world hike. Even in the moments I hate him, I can still see what drew Mom to him.

Dad's decision to move out at the beginning of my senior year was strategic, calculated to catch both Mom and me off guard. It worked, too. We were both so caught up in the new academic year that we couldn't summon the energy to instigate any fights or even proffer a few choice—and wholly justified—profanities. The only sign he'd gone at all was the sudden feeling of emptiness and quietness. And a note that said he'd left for good and we could keep everything—he wouldn't be needing it. It wasn't meant to be kind; it meant that wherever he was going, and whoever the woman was, things were looking up for him.

I immediately took down all the pictures of Dad, but Mom put them all back up again. I told her not to e-mail him or leave messages on his cell phone, but she did both anyway. Everyone remotely close to her told her to let go, to not appear desperate. But she *was* desperate. Improbably, after all he'd done, she still loved him. And it's pretty clear she still does.

I notice that Mom has also changed the photo beside Dad's. In place of the fixed-smile, arms-locked husband-and-wife portrait taken three Christmases ago, she's put up that old black-and-white photo of herself that was taken in grad school: the bohemian scholar in a hand-knitted poncho, tousled black hair tucked haphazardly behind multiply pierced ears. It was the photo above her bio when she published her first book on the origins of the suffragette movement, although it was totally out-of-date by then. Even now, I think that's the woman she would like to see staring back at her whenever she looks in the mirror.

Seeing the photos side by side reminds me that there was a time when my parents were a reasonably attractive couple—stylish even, in a knowingly subversive way. They were an energetic pair back then too: "free spirits joined in an intoxicating quest for love and excitement" is how Mom puts it. I guess that's the idea of their marriage she has decided to memorialize every time she walks up the stairs and passes this spot. It's sad, but I can understand it. The young couple in the photos seems capable of a romance that their modern-day counterparts weren't able to sustain.

Maybe one day I'll understand how someone like Dad gets everything, and someone like Mom is left with nothing. Maybe there's some divine justice at the end of the road, but if there is, I don't see any signs of it yet. All I can see is that nice guys really do finish last, and that's an area where I have much more in common with Mom than with Dad. I don't want to finish last. I want to experience the kind of passion that my parents once enjoyed. Only I won't mess it up when I find it.

Two hours later, I remove the lasagna because the smoke seeping out of the oven has set off the alarm. It's no longer recognizable—it's a lasagna only in spirit.

I call Matt the Mutt over and tip the entire dish into his bowl, even the charred bits stuck to the side; it's not like he won't eat them, after all. He gives me a wonderfully gratifying look that says, *you're the best, Kev*, which feels good because most of the time he pretty much hates me. Then he takes a mouthful and starts howling the place down. He dunks his snout into the water bowl and leaves it there until his tongue stops burning. Then he gives me a horribly disconcerting look that says, *you're a butthole, Kev, and don't be surprised if I accidentally soil on your new Abercrombie & Fitch sweatshirt.*

I'm about to go and pick my sweatshirt off the floor when Mom runs into the kitchen.

"What did you do to the dog?"

"Nothing. I just gave him the lasagna."

"Oh, that." Mom had clearly forgotten about it too. "It comes out pretty hot, you know."

"Yeah. I didn't think he'd eat it right away."

Matt circles my ankles like he's biding his time before exacting—or, more likely, excreting—revenge.

"Look, Mom, I'm sorry I asked you about Dad."

"It's okay. You must miss him."

"Yeah," I say reflexively, then remember that it's not entirely true. "Well, no. Not really."

Mom steps forward and hugs me. "It's okay to miss him, you know."

I can't decide whether her remark is directed toward me or if she's really giving herself permission to mourn his absence. Maybe we really do need to work on being more open with each other, more communicative.

I want to ask her about the photos upstairs. I want to show her that I notice these things, that I care, but I don't know how to broach difficult topics subtly anymore. All I can do is resort to small gestures like putting down the toilet seat to show that I'm different from Dad. She was quite proud of me when I started doing that.

Then again, maybe now isn't the best time to usher in a new era of openness. Mom would certainly be a lot less proud of me if she found out about the Graduation Rituals, which are not exactly in line with her belief system. Telling her that the senior girls don't object wouldn't help either. And if she discovers that I'm compiling the Book of Busts, I may as well emigrate. My body stiffens just thinking about it.

Mom pulls away. "Kevin, I think it's only fair to tell you that I got a call from Ms. Kowalski today . . ."

All righty, so she already knows about the Rituals. I guess I should start packing.

"I don't want to talk about this, Mom."

"But I think it's important that we talk about it. Get everything out in the open before things become complicated."

I want to point out that things wouldn't be complicated if Ms. Kowalski hadn't called. I can't believe she ratted me out to my own mother.

"Look, Mom. I just want to have some space at school…do what I want to do, you know?"

"Okay. I can understand that."

"You can?"

"Sure. Now can we please discuss Ms. Kowalski's call?"

"No."

"I thought you said you wanted to communicate."

"So did you," I mutter defensively. "But you still haven't told me what Dad's e-mail said."

It's a cheap shot, and I regret it immediately. Mom looks deflated as she backs away toward the door. She mumbles good night without looking at me, and it's not until she's gone that I notice it's still only eight o'clock.

This business of not talking seems to require saying some really mean things.

Abby calls me an hour later, and I'm glad. She has a unique ability to make me feel like a halfway-decent human being, even when all signs point to the contrary.

"What're you up to?" she asks.

"Just sitting here, finishing some reading for tomorrow."

"Not, like, a book?"

"Yeah. Most of our reading comes in the form of books, Abby. I thought you knew that."

"Ha ha. You know what I mean. Is it a novel?"

"Yeah, it's a novel."

Abby sighs like this is a Big Deal, which it kind of is to her. English is not her finest class, and she claims that novels bore her. She prefers mathematical equations and the periodic table because they're shorter. I think she has a fear of commitment to anything longer than a page.

"Do you need any help with math?"

"No, that's okay. I got it," I lie.

"You're just saying that 'cause you don't want me to come over."

"That's not true. Although it does seem kind of dumb to be talking on the phone. I mean, I can see you from my window."

"No you can't," she laughs. "I'm on the far side of my bedroom. And anyway, my blind is closed."

I peek out my window at the upstairs bedroom of the house next door. Sure enough, her blind is closed. But then it opens, and she's standing there in a revealing slip that shines in the amber glow from a table lamp. She's less than twenty feet away. I draw my breath in suddenly, then remember that she can hear me.

"Can you see me now?" she says provocatively, eyeing me the whole time.

"Yeah."

"Hmmm. And how do I look?"

She looks good. Actually, she looks beautiful, but I don't

dare say that and I'm afraid she can see my cheeks are burning, so I step back from the window.

"You know," I say, stalling, "I think we call each other so we can pretend we're not going to end up talking for an hour, even though we always do."

She laughs politely, but I can tell it's not what she wanted to hear. By the time I look up again she's closed her blind.

"What was wrong this afternoon, Kev? You seemed weird after practice."

"Nothing was wrong."

"Are you sure?"

"Yeah, I just... I'm just afraid people at the prom won't think our music's cool."

She groans. "You've got to stop worrying about what other people think is cool. If you enjoy it, why do you care what they think?"

"You're right, I know, but it worries me, that's all. I can't help it."

"Listen. For what it's worth, I think you're so much cooler than them."

"Who?"

"The people you're afraid won't find the music cool. You know, Brandon and his gang. Really, you're cooler and smarter and funnier than they'll ever be. And I can't tell you how pleased I am that you're not like them."

Our calls always seem to end like this, with Abby complimenting me. Only this time it's not so reassuring. Because as I close my cell phone, it occurs to me that I *am* one of them.

8

I'm sitting at a baseball game and Brookbank High is winning. Actually, we're winning by so much that the score resembles that of a football game, but that's normal. Brookbank's team is legendary, and each year the coach parlays his city championship into yet another pay raise. This year will be no different.

It's a warm, late-spring evening and there's a pretty good crowd here, which enables me to stay hidden at the back of the bleachers. I don't want anybody to speak to me because they'll just ask me why I'm here, and then I'll have to admit that Brandon and the rest of the team coerced me into coming.

We're between innings, and Brandon's current girl of choice, Morgan, is taking her role as cheerleading captain very seriously. Starved of anything to cheer about all year—all our other teams suck—she encourages the cheerleaders to cavort wildly on the sidelines, inciting the crowd to attempt the wave. A couple of senior guys are game and jump out of their seats, spraying Red Bull all over the spectators around them. By the time the game resumes, they've been escorted out of the ballpark.

Brandon steps up to bat, looking like a blond-haired Derek Jeter. Like his idol, he plays shortstop. In Brandon's case, the position is rich in sexual symbolism: he's splitting his time between second and third bases, a grope here and a dry hump there. And that's just when he's being defensive. Put him on the offense and his ability to hit home runs is legendary. Ask any girl.

He hits a home run on the first pitch, and the scoreboard tilts even more heavily in favor of our team. Brandon bows his head modestly and begins a steady jog around the bases. As he passes second, he glances up and winks at Morgan, who claps her hands appreciatively. I can't help wondering if Brandon's choice of second base is symbolic, a way of communicating his intention to get under her shirt tonight. If so, Morgan is either blissfully ignorant or ecstatic about it.

As Brandon reaches home plate, the announcer explains that with a difference of fifteen runs the mercy rule will be applied and the game is over. It's only the fifth inning. I can't believe my luck. I decide to run home so I can go to Abby's and catch a movie, but then I hear Brandon calling to me:

"Kev, we're hitting IHOP. It's kind of lame, but Ryan's dating one of the waitresses so we always get free stuff. Spud'll give you a ride."

I'm about to make an excuse when Morgan sidles up to Brandon and starts fawning over him. He places a hand behind her head and pulls her forward, and within seconds they're tonguing with Olympic intensity.

"Dude. Like. Whoa."

Spud stands beside me, and in spite of his monosyllabic conversational skills, I can't help feeling I have a lot more in common with him than with Brandon.

"I guess we'll have Morgan's scores by Monday," I say under my breath.

Spud nods. "Dude."

✦

On the way to IHOP I seriously begin to question my transition to Brookbank's social elite. After all, while I'm riding shotgun with Spud in his sputtering Chevy Nova, wondering what's holding all the pieces of rust together, Brandon's riding shotgun with Morgan in her Miata, probably scanning through the tracks on her iPod until he finds the right make-out song. I'm no expert, but these seem like the polar extremes of coolness, and right now I'm definitely on the wrong end.

Spud's car stalls at the entrance to the IHOP parking lot. As we push it into a disabled parking space, I have the unsettling feeling that I was more hip when I was just a geeky flutist. I've gone from bad to worse—a classic Mopsely maneuver.

Inside, the baseball team has commandeered a few booths, but everyone fights to share Brandon's table. He doesn't seem to notice, since he's busy giving Morgan one last tongue. Then he pats her on the butt and sends her packing to the cheerleaders' booth. As I follow Spud toward a mostly empty booth, I hear Brandon calling me over to join him.

"But there's no room," Zach scowls, as soon as he sees me.

"Are you sure about that?" says Brandon. "Because if there isn't, you're going to need to move. Kev's my guest of honor." He punches my arm in ritualistic greeting.

Zach shifts a few inches, grumbling under his breath. I sit down gingerly and glance at the baseball players across from me. They all have that sheen of sweaty masculinity, even though most of them never broke into a jog the whole game.

"What can I get you boys?" asks a kind-looking woman, her face a tangle of laugh lines.

"Well, for a start you can get us a waitress who's under sixty," mutters Zach. "Grab Keira." He points across the table at Ryan. "This guy's banging her at the moment."

The woman blinks a few times. She looks as though she's about to say something, but instead she just studies each of our faces like she's memorizing details for the voodoo dolls she plans to make later.

"What was that all about?" muses Brandon, as soon as she leaves.

"Weird," comments Zach profoundly.

Moments later Keira sidles up to our table, flushed red with embarrassment.

"Hey, Ryan," she whispers, then bites her lower lip nervously and fiddles with her paper pad.

"Hey, babe," Ryan bellows. "How much free shit'll you be able to get us tonight?"

Keira spins around like she's expecting to find the manager beside her taking notes.

"I don't know, okay? It's not easy. And now you've upset Janet, and she's the manager's wife, so I'll have to be real careful."

Ryan shakes his head disgustedly. "Whatever. Don't do us any favors or nothing. I'm just your boyfriend, that's all. Nothing special."

"Oh, Ryan, I'm sorry. I'll take care of it, okay? Food's on me tonight. I'll pay out of my tips."

Keira takes our orders, but I can't bear to ask for anything. Ryan notices and orders the most expensive item on the menu for me. Keira winces, then leaves.

"That was good, man," applauds Zach, chinking his glass of water against Ryan's. "Do you even like this chick, or is it just about the free food?"

"Some of both, you know?"

Zach nods and crunches an ice cube loudly between his teeth.

"Hey, guys," says Paige, venturing over from the cheerleaders' booth. "Whassup?"

Paige Tramell is hot and she knows it. She's tied her blond hair back in two long pigtails that scream *I'm-cute-and-I'm-innocent!* and she's changed into a bright white crop top (she always dresses in white to be ironic) that shows off her belly button ring. All the guys stare unblinkingly at her tummy, but she pretends not to notice, so I figure she doesn't mind. I look too.

"Haven't seen you here before, Kevin," she says.

I feel my head jerking back up to her face. "No, I…"

"He's one of us now," says Brandon, wrapping a muscled arm around me. "Trust me, Kevin's big time."

"Oh yeah?" Paige's brows knit momentarily, but then she smiles and bites her lip in a really sexy way. "I'll have to remember that," she says, tapping her finger against her head. "That's the kind of thing a girl ought to know, Kevin."

Just to hear her say my name makes my legs go to Jell-O. I try to think of something to say, but my mouth just flaps open and shut a few times like a fish starved of oxygen. Eventually I look away. I know it's a dorky response, but I don't care. I want to bottle this moment and keep it for the rest of my life.

I've officially entered the ranks of the cool.

9

I'm trying not to ogle Morgan and Taylor, but it's diffi-cult. They're sitting on either side of me, forming a Kevin sandwich with their pretty faces and beautiful breasts. As they lean over our shared table in a way that reminds me how truly feminine they are, I worry that my hard-on won't wear off before class ends. But then I realize what a won-derful problem that is to have, and offer a silent prayer of thanks to Brandon.

While she waits for everyone to calm down—which always takes up the first ten minutes of every English class— Ms. Kowalski glares at our unlikely trio. If she were a guy I'd say she's just jealous of me, but instead I assume this is all related to the Graduation Rituals. I never realized how much it would bug her. And I certainly never guessed she'd call my mom. I don't think that Ms. K and I are best bud-dies anymore.

For most of class Ms. K monologues on everything from Sylvia Plath to split infinitives, and the room gets progressively quieter. Eventually she runs out of steam, sits down, and rummages through her notes.

"All right," she says with forced enthusiasm, "in honor of our baseball team's recent success, I'd like to discuss your favorite sports movies."

"*Friday Night Lights*," shouts Ryan, whose status as one of the pitchers for the victorious team makes him well-qualified to speak without raising his hand. "It's got everything...guys hitting each other, career-ending injuries, domestic violence."

Beside me, Taylor tuts disapprovingly. "What a profound basis for a movie." Even when she's pissed, her voice is rich and sexy.

"You just don't understand it 'cause you're a girl."

"Another profound observation."

"Now, now," interjects Ms. K, "I think what Ryan's saying is that he appreciates the way these movies affirm his masculinity. Isn't that right, Ryan?"

Ryan stares at her blankly. I think the tiny part of his brain that still functions is gradually turning to mush.

"Ryan?"

It's painfully amusing to watch Ryan stare. If it goes on long enough he may start bleeding from his ears. That would be kind of cool.

"Ryan? Do you think that's reasonable?" Ms. K repeats, an encouraging smile pasted on her face.

Ryan continues his audition for the waxworks museum,

and eventually Ms. K looks kind of freaked out. She turns to the rest of the class.

"Anyone else got a favorite sports film?" she says with decidedly less enthusiasm.

Morgan raises her hand, and as she does her hair brushes against my arm. It's soft and smells citrus-y, and it glints in the brightness of the room, and I suddenly have no idea what she's saying.

"That's a good example, Morgan," Ms. K commends her. "I'm sure we've all seen *A League of Their Own*. But what's the appeal?"

"Are you kidding?" gasps Paige from her customary seat at the back of the room. "There's the cute cast, for a start. Like, Geena Davis before she got old—hot chick. Madonna before she got pregnant—hot chick. And Tom Hanks has got to be the most adorable drunk guy in, like, forever. And even the fat chick gets to be funny, so she's cool too."

Taylor sighs. "Maybe that's why no one takes women's sports seriously. They're just interested in whether the women are cute or funny."

"Which is why cheerleading is so important," says Morgan earnestly. "It shows everyone we're athletic as well."

"Yeah, great. We stand on the sidelines cheering on the boys. And even then, nobody watches us."

She's wrong about that, but it's probably not cool for me to admit that whenever I'm forced to attend games I spend the whole time ogling the cheerleaders.

"That's an excellent point, Taylor." Ms. K claps her hands together. "And quite relevant to what our special guest has come to say."

Everyone seems as surprised as I am that there's a guest, and that they'd arrive only five minutes before the end of class.

"As you're probably aware," Ms. K continues, "you have little more than a month of school left. And since it's no secret that we don't give a final exam at the end of senior year, I decided it might be preferable to some of you to broaden your horizons. So, for the rest of the semester, you'll have the option to attend either my class or a class that focuses on women's issues in modern society—like equal opportunities, and sexism, and feminism. It'll be taught by a professor from Brookbank University, and it's open to everyone—"

Ryan snorts loudly, a characteristically intellectual contribution. But I'm not snorting. I'm taking deep breaths, trying to remain calm.

"—She's an inspirational teacher, and will get you thinking about these issues in ways you may never have imagined. I'd recommend it to all of you, but obviously it's optional." Ms. K looks out to the corridor and beckons the professor in. "I'd like you all to give a big Brookbank welcome to Dr. Maggie Donaldson."

Dr. Maggie Donaldson enters hurriedly, shakes Ms. Kowalski's hand, then scans the room. She doesn't make eye contact with me, but I look away anyway. I don't need to watch her to know how she looks: she's wearing her silvery hair long because she thinks it looks distinguished, when really it just makes her look old; her bright red fingernail polish is spotty because she bites her nails; she's wearing a long flowery dress with sewn-on satin flowers that her mother bought during a family pilgrimage to San Francisco for the "summer of love," 1967. Even though it barely hangs together, she says it's her favorite dress.

I look around the room at the other students, expecting to see them making faces at one another—if anyone in history is ripe for a Brookbank High crucifixion, it's her. But no one is laughing. Instead, they're hanging on her every word because she's a college professor, not a teacher. She's the most unfashionable person they've ever seen and she keeps using words most of them won't understand, but they respect her anyway.

For the first time in my life, I am truly jealous of my mom.

10

At the first opportunity, all the guys sprint away like they're being chased. Meanwhile, I wait at the back of the room as one by one the girls step forward to sign up for the new class. As they leave, each one casts a nervous glance in my direction, obviously thinking I'd be nuts to sign up for a class on Women's Studies.

They have no idea how right they are.

Eventually only Ms. Kowalski and my mom and me remain, and Ms. K is smirking triumphantly. It's like she's declared war on me and is savoring an early, decisive victory.

"Thanks so much, Dr. Donaldson."

Mom snorts. "Please, call me Maggie. I think we can do away with formal titles now, can't we?"

Ms. K looks unsure. "Okay...Maggie. But seriously, thanks. I just know this'll be a positive experience for everyone."

"Oh, it's my pleasure, Jane," replies Mom.

Jane? I don't think I ever realized that the J in Ms. J. Kowalski actually stood for anything.

"Jane was one of the finest students I ever taught at Brookbank," Mom explains to me. "But I've probably told you that many times, right?"

Huh? No, she has not told me that many times. In fact, she's never even mentioned that Ms. K was a student of hers. This is cruel and unusual.

"Well," says Ms. K amiably, "I'll leave you two to … to …" She blushes, then tries to salvage a graceful exit by speeding away.

"I hadn't realized so many of your classmates would be interested in my class," Mom exclaims. "Isn't it wonderful?"

"Yeah, great. But don't think I'll be coming."

She laughs. "I wouldn't expect you to. If you don't understand these issues after living with me for eighteen years, then it's probably too late anyway. But Jane seems to think that there are some boys in the senior class who are enforcing unattainable and repugnant ideals of femininity, and she really doesn't want any of the girls to fall afoul of their particular brand of ideological misogyny."

Okay, so that's how you know my mom's a professor, because she can conjure phrases like "ideological misogyny" without stuttering or pausing to draw her breath. It's strangely impressive and mesmerizing. And it's just dawning on me that the people she's referring to are Brandon Trent's gang. And that includes me.

Then Mom's smile disappears, replaced by a look of concern. "What's the matter?"

"Huh?"

"Come on. You think I can't tell when you're angry?"

"I'm not angry," I lie.

"Okay, although—"

"All right, then, yeah, I'm angry. How could you do this without telling me?"

Mom carefully places the list of names into her hemp shoulder bag. "I tried to tell you, but you wouldn't listen."

"When?"

"Last week. I told you Ms. Kowalski had called me, and you told me you just wanted some space at school. And I'll give you space, don't worry."

"So this is what she called you about—doing the class?"

"Yes, obviously. Why else would she call?"

I gulp. "Um, no reason."

"Kevin, please. I know that something's going on here. Let's just get it all out in the open, okay?"

It's tempting. I've never been good at keeping secrets from Mom, but telling her about the Book of Busts would be equivalent to announcing I've joined a Satanic cult.

"There's nothing else," I assure her. "I just hadn't expected to see you here. It's a shock, that's all."

She leans forward and kisses me on the cheek. "Well, don't worry. I don't want to embarrass you or make your life complicated. You won't even know I'm here!"

Mom saunters off with a lightness of step that I find completely inappropriate and quite enviable.

I'm feeling out of my depth, so I do what I always do when things spiral out of control: I call Abby. She has caller ID, so I know she'll pick up the phone after a single ring. Sure enough, the line clicks to life, but before I can speak her voice erupts on the other end:

"Isn't it wonderful, your mom teaching the Women's Studies course?"

How does she know about that?

"How do you know about that?"

"Because she came into my English class and introduced herself. It's not just your class that's invited to take her course, you know."

"I wasn't saying that—"

"I think it's so cool what she's doing," Abby bubbles. "I'm definitely going to go. The way I see it, Brandon and his pack of lap dogs have gotten away with their sexist agenda for long enough."

I can't believe how like my mom she sounds. It's actually kind of scary.

"Did you hear me, Kev?"

"Yeah."

"And don't you agree?"

"Uh…"

She coughs meaningfully. "What's going on?"

"What do you mean? Nothing's going on."

"Kevin…"

I take a deep breath. "Look, if I tell you, do you promise not to give me a hard time?"

"No."

"Oh, okay… Um, well, you know Brandon's meeting

the other day? I sort of, did go to it, actually and ... well, it's kind of like I'm ... sort of ... involved."

Abby treats me to a lengthy silence before mumbling, "You're kidding me, right?"

"Well ... " Oh geez. Even now I'm tempted to lie to her and pretend that yeah, I'm kidding. "No, I'm not kidding."

"But why?"

"Because I didn't know what the meeting was about. I had no way of knowing what I was getting into."

"Crikey, Kev, your mom'll brain you if she finds out. Or she'll just cut you off, or cut you up, or throw you out and disown you—"

"This is not helping, Abby."

"Sorry, but it's true. Looking on the bright side, at least nobody but me knows she's your mom. I'd forgotten she goes by her maiden name, and it was pretty clear no one knew who she was. Even Nathan and Caitlin didn't recognize her."

I hadn't considered this. "That could be a lifesaver."

"For now, sure. But it's only a matter of time before someone makes the connection."

"Maybe."

"No maybe about it. It'll happen, and when it does she'll castrate you—"

"Abby!"

"I'm just saying ... You know what you have to do, right? You've got to face those guys and say 'no, I won't be involved in this.' This isn't who you are, Kevin. Brandon's an asshole. You're not."

"Why do you hate him so much?"

"Let's just say I have my reasons."

"Like what?"

Silence. I can hear Abby breathing heavily. "Freshman year, he asked me out."

"What?"

"It was just his little joke. He had his entourage with him, and I knew he wasn't serious. And I wouldn't have dated him even if he had been. But I felt so ... powerless, you know? Knowing I was about to become the butt of his joke and there was nothing I could do about it. If I said yes, he'd just laugh. If I said no, he'd say he wasn't serious anyway. So I didn't say anything. After a few seconds he smiled and told me not to stress about it, that he'd get over it soon. He looked so serious you'd almost believe he meant it, except that behind him all his cronies were snickering like it was the funniest thing they'd ever heard. The whole thing only lasted a moment, and I don't think any of them ever thought about it again. But I've never forgotten."

"Why didn't you tell me before?"

"Why do you think? Because it was humiliating."

"But that's just Brandon being Brandon. He doesn't mean anything by it."

More silence, and this time I can't even hear her breathing. "Oh. I see."

"I'm not saying it was a nice thing to do, Abby—"

"Please, Kevin," she says suddenly, earnestly. "Please believe me. You don't want to be like them." She hesitates, swallows hard. "And I don't want you to be like them."

She says it so kindly, so tenderly, that I feel grateful to

her in spite of her earlier forecasts of dismemberment and castration.

I walk over to my bedroom window and look out. I see Abby's face framed by her bedroom window, her hair draped loosely over her shoulders, a halo glowing around her from the light behind. Her eyes appear moist, but it's probably just a trick of the light. As I continue to gaze at her, it's like I'm looking at an angel. And although I know she's not everybody's idea of beautiful, right now I can't help feeling that she might be mine.

11

I avoid Ms. Kowalski's gaze throughout English, which isn't hard to do as I'm sitting next to Paige Tramell.

Yes, *Paige Tramell!*

I was waiting to see if I might get lucky with Morgan and Taylor again when Paige just plopped down next to me and began talking. She said how weird it was to have that professor come in yesterday, and how she'd never join a Women's Studies class like some of the other girls, and if they weren't all so freakin' ugly they wouldn't need feminism, and anyway the professor looked like a bag lady.

We launch into an extended critique of Mom's flowery dress, at which point Ms. K asks us to shut up or enjoy detention together. Paige just rolls her eyes at me and rubs my leg, and for the second time in two days I wonder if my hard-on will wear off before I have to stand up.

At the end of class, Paige leans in and places a hand on

my knee. "Look," she says. "I understand if you're not interested, but I'd really like to go on a date with you."

"…"

"I said, I'd like to go on a date with you."

I'm so shocked that I can't actually speak, which makes the conversation somewhat stilted.

Paige waits a few seconds, then shakes her head mournfully. "I understand if you don't find me attractive. I'd just really hoped that maybe you might find me … bearable," she chokes.

I'm still struggling to locate my vocal cords, but eventually I manage: "I do … find you bearable."

Bearable? Did I really just say that?

"Oh, that's such a relief." She visibly relaxes. "Then let's call it a date for this evening, okay?"

"Uh … sure." I nod vacantly. "Hold on, *this* evening?"

"Yeah. 'Cause, you know, you might be busy after tonight."

I don't know why she'd think that, but I'm not dumb enough to blow an opportunity like this. "Okay. Sure."

"Great. Let's meet at El Pollo Loco at five, okay?"

I'm about to agree, but Paige has already left the room.

Before the Graduation Rituals meeting I make a quick pit stop in the boys' bathroom to practice my reluctant-yet-decisive resignation speech. I know I told Brandon that I was committed, but I can't take on Abby, Ms. K, *and* my mom—I'm simply not strong enough. Anyway, the guys will probably be pleased to get rid of me. I run through my spiel one more time, turning my palms up like a martyred saint and furrowing my eyebrows like I'm constipated. Now that I've nailed the right look, I'm ready.

My confidence is short-lived. As I approach the meeting room, I feel my pulse quickening. Doing the right thing is okay in theory, but in practice I'm running the risk of pissing off Brookbank's most volatile group, which seems like an oddly self-destructive course of action. To make matters worse, I notice that everybody else has already arrived. I take a deep breath, but before I've even walked through the door they all rise and applaud me.

"Kev Mopsely, you dog," barks Brandon. "Hooking up with Paige Tramell already!"

"Well, I haven't technically hooked up with her yet—"

"She's a total babe," adds Ryan, completely ignoring my interruption. "I mean, she's flat-chested as a ten-year-old boy, but man, that butt. And what about those lips." Ryan performs the universal jerk-off sign.

"But just remember," Brandon reminds me, "it's the numbers we're after, not a grade for how good a kisser she is. Got it?"

All eyes are on me, so I nod meekly.

"Oh, and before you leave today," Brandon says in a suddenly serious voice, "Chase has some numbers for you to add to the Book of Busts. Sounds like he was pretty busy this weekend, taking one for the team. Or was it two or three, Chase?"

I almost wish I didn't understand what he means by that,

but as everyone else is laughing, I laugh too. By the time the laughter subsides, I realize that I haven't yet resigned. And I know I can't, either.

✦

Mom is still at work when I get home, so I have to call her to say I'm going out on a date. It makes me feel like I'm thirteen.

"That's great, honey." Mom's voice explodes across the line. "I've been hoping you two would finally get around to having a date."

Whoa, that was unexpected. "Who? Me and Paige?"

"Who?"

"Paige Tramell."

"Who's she?"

"A friend of mine."

Silence. "Oh, you've never mentioned her before."

"Yeah, well … she's a, er, friend," I mumble.

"Yes, I get that." Another pause. "So what's she like? I mean, how do you know her? Is she a musician?"

"No."

"Is she a good student?"

"Not especially."

"Have I ever met her?"

"No."

"Huh … I know it's none of my business, honey, but exactly why are you going on a date with her?"

How did informing my mom I'd be late home suddenly segue into the third degree about my love life?

"It's just a date, Mom. Okay? That's all. It doesn't mean anything."

Another silence. "Hmmm. That's a shame."

"Why?"

"Well, because anytime you really like someone, a date means something," explains Mom in her I'm-so-patient voice. "It means a whole lot, in fact."

"Geez. Why are you making this such a big deal?"

"I'm not, honey, I'm not. I mean, sure, go out and have fun. You deserve it."

I picture her shaking her head disappointedly as she hangs up, then kneeling down and putting a hex on my date with Paige.

As if it needs one.

12

Paige is talking. A lot. And most of what spills out of her mouth is too inane for me to remember even a moment later. But I don't care, because Paige is so hot she could recite the alphabet incorrectly and I'd still gaze at her like she'd won me over with a heartfelt Shakespearean sonnet.

She's wearing a white halter top, and her blond hair is down so that it cascades over her shoulders in loving waves. I want to touch her hair so badly. I also want to touch her tummy, and her face, and pretty much every other part of her. But I don't tell her this because I don't want her to run away.

"So anyway," Paige grinds on, "I told Caitlin to get a life. And I said that while she was at it she ought to realize that Goths wear black. I mean, what a total loser."

"She's allergic to black clothes dye," I explain, then remember that I'm in a purely observational role here.

"Oh. How'd you know that?"

"I play in a quartet with her."

Paige nods deeply. "Okay, that's worth knowing. So you're, like, friends with her?"

The question seems loaded, so I hesitate. "Yeah, I guess so."

Paige nods again. "Right. That's worth knowing too."

She's clearly eager to order some food, but it's almost impossible to signal to a waiter since we're stuck at the very back of the restaurant, in a secluded booth miles from the nearest diners. I was really bummed when Paige asked for this booth specifically, as it meant no one would see me with her, and part of the pleasure of having a date with someone as hot as Paige is being seen with her in public.

"God, are we ever going to get served?" she moans. "Seriously, do you find the service in Mexican restaurants always sucks?"

"No, I don't," I admit, chomping down on a tortilla chip loaded with salsa.

She flinches as I eat, and it occurs to me that she hasn't had any yet.

"So Mexicans don't bother you?" she asks, composing herself.

"No, of course not."

"What about Asians?"

"No."

"Okay, that's useful to know."

A waiter appears before I have a chance to ask her how on earth that's a useful piece of information. Paige orders a taco salad, and I get chicken in a mole sauce. As soon as the waiter leaves, I have visions of brownish gunk smeared all over my shirt and pants and wish I'd had the sense to order something more manageable.

Paige shuffles in her seat across from me. "So, do you find it cute when girls act all shy and reserved, or do you prefer it when they just come on strong?"

Hmmm, tricky one. With a prior sample size of zero, it's hard for me to say. Except that I'm a guy, so it's actually quite easy.

"S-Strong. Definitely strong."

Paige narrows her eyes. "Good. Good to know. And do you prefer to start off with kissing, or … " She trails off, waiting for me to fill in the blank.

"Um … kissing's good."

She nods and brushes her hand across her bare tummy. "That's good to know."

Again I'm intrigued by the number of things I say that are good to know. But I don't spend much time contemplating the matter, since Paige stands up and comes over to my side of the booth.

"So, do you like it when girls just take the initiative and … you know?"

I'm about to die, but it'll be a fantastic way to go.

"Yeah … I like that."

Paige smiles. She leans in toward me and plants her lips gently on my cheek, then my other cheek, then the area just beside my mouth, and then …

My lips. I'm not sure if she actually wants me to kiss her back, and when I do absolutely nothing for several seconds she stops and looks concerned.

"Is it okay?"

"Oh God, yes."

"Good to know."

She leans in again, and this time starts straight in on the lips. As she pushes gently against me I let my mouth open and my tongue—

"Fuck!" she says, pulling back suddenly.

"What?"

"Huh? Oh, nothing. It's just... you need to go gently, you know? Let the kissing be all close-mouthed for a while, then move on. Got it?"

I nod. Paige takes a deep breath, readies herself, then leans in again. This time we hang around the general vicinity of each other's lips for a good long time, and I don't open my mouth until she opens hers, and I don't pop my tongue inside until her tongue gently finds mine, at which point I don't hold anything back—

"Shit!" exclaims Paige, then collects herself. "Kevin, listen... you have to be gentle with tongues. This isn't about staking a claim to my mouth, it's about slowly exploring the tip of my tongue. If that's good, move on to another part of the tongue, but never use your own like a fucking Mack truck."

Maybe it's not such a bad thing that our booth is separated from the rest of the diners.

Paige takes another deep breath and leans forward again. We resume kissing from where we left off, and I do what she says and it's actually really good, even though her mouth tastes like an ashtray. It's almost like she's done this a lot, because she certainly knows what she's talking about. After a while we part naturally, and Paige is smiling.

"Not bad, Kevin. You should definitely avoid the salsa in the future, but other than that there's hope for you."

It's kind of a backhanded compliment, but I don't really care because I just French-kissed Paige Tramell, and this is definitely better than any fantasy I've ever had.

Paige leans back against the booth cushions and runs her fingers all the way through her hair. When she reaches the tips she moves her hands to her breasts, then realizes what she's done and looks embarrassed.

"Oops. I just touched myself," she giggles. "Hey, you'll never believe what happened to me today."

"What?" I hope it has something to do with her touching her breasts.

"I found out I have the same physical measurements as Jessica Alba. Isn't that an amazing coincidence? Someone said they'd found out her measurements from some movie Web site, and when I went and looked, they were exactly the same."

"That's cool," I mumble, but all I can think about is how I've just managed to get Paige's entry for the Book of Busts on our first date. And she doesn't even realize what she's told me.

"Yeah, funny," Paige says. She moves back to her side of the booth as the food arrives.

The waiter has barely finished arranging the plates neatly before us when Paige asks to have hers boxed since she has cheerleading practice in half an hour.

"You *what?*"

"I have cheerleading practice. I told you." She pauses. "Didn't I tell you?" She looks genuinely horrified at having omitted this rather crucial detail. "I'm so sorry, Kevin. Now you must feel like this date has been the biggest waste of your time."

"But...you've still got a few minutes, haven't you? I mean, if you don't need to be there for half an hour."

"No, I really gotta go. I need to smoke three cigarettes before practice. I read that most supermodels smoke a pack a day to keep their weight down, so I'm trying to catch up."

"But you do cheerleading. Doesn't that keep your weight down?"

"Screw cheerleading. I'm only in it 'cause the baseball final will be televised, and that's when I'll be spotted by a talent agency."

Huh. Vacuous *and* conniving. Cool.

"So what's with the patch?" I ask, pointing to the square on her arm.

Paige glances at it. "Oh, my dad got upset when he found out I smoke. I wear this so he knows I'm really trying to quit." She doesn't seem terribly bothered by the duplicity.

The waiter reappears with Paige's box. She conjures a sad face for me, bites her lip remorsefully, then leans over and plants another moist kiss on my lips. By the time she leaves, I almost don't mind her going. I've got just about everything I could ever have hoped for from a first date.

Even the check seems like a small price to pay for such wild success.

13

Luckily Mom stays late at work, so I don't have to explain why I'm home so soon. Her absence also gives me a chance to use the computer to conduct some quick Web research.

Measurements Jessica Alba.

Google announces a number of useful hits, and moments later I'm jotting down incredibly private information about Jessica Alba. I don't exactly know how the site got hold of the figures—I can't imagine Jessica Alba volunteered them—but there they are, big and bold: 34B-24-34.

Mom's always telling me what a wonderful educational resource the Internet is, but until now I can't say I believed her. I scan the list of other famous actresses whose figures are listed; there are even revealing photographs of some of them conveniently located just a click away.

I click.

This may be the most momentous evening of my life. I'm already imagining the next Rituals meeting, contemplating how I'll present my findings to the guys. I even start to wonder if they'll kneel down before me, which is probably why I don't hear the door opening—

"Hi, honey. How'd it go tonight?"

I try to close the photograph as soon as it begins to emerge, but a little disk is floating around telling me the computer is occupied.

"Honey?"

"It w-was fine," I say, or attempt to say; it comes out garbled on account of the fact that a naked woman is gradually being revealed on the computer screen.

"So what exactly *were* you doing tonight?" asks—

"Abby!" I gasp, spinning around. "What are you doing here?"

Abby points at the monitor. "What's that?"

I look back at the screen, but thankfully the computer has decided it actually has time to close the window after all. "Nothing. Nothing at all," I say, wiping sweat off my forehead.

Abby shrugs. "So you were going to tell me what you were doing tonight."

I look at Mom. "I, er, had a meeting."

Mom raises her eyebrows but leaves without contradicting me. Abby watches her go, then closes the door softly.

"So listen, I just wanted to come around to ask, well, you know ... how it went."

"What do you mean?"

"Oh, come on. I know who you met with today."

I swallow hard. "You do?"

"Yeah, I do... Don't act so surprised. It's not exactly a secret."

"It isn't?"

"No, you twit, it isn't. So, go on, did you do it?"

"Did I *what!?*" I can feel myself go bright red, and suddenly I really don't want to be here having this conversation with Abby.

"Did you, you know... do it?" repeats Abby without a hint of embarrassment.

"Um, I... well, I really don't see how it's any of your business."

Abby looks flabbergasted, like I've just landed a sucker punch in her gut.

"Okay, okay. No, I didn't *do* it," I assure her.

"What?" Now she looks even more horrified, which is really freaky. "Why not? Weren't you up to it? Or, I know," she adds testily, "maybe you just don't have the balls for it."

That's the last straw. "If you must know, yes, I do have the balls for it, but it's up to me whether or not I decide to do it, and it's certainly got nothing to do with you."

Abby cocks her head, stares at me with narrowed eyes. "Okay, I get it," she says softly, her head nodding imperceptibly. "I guess I'll go now." She turns to leave, then pauses before the door. "Although, I want you to know that I only came here because I care about you. And don't think I don't know how difficult it must be to stand up to Brandon and his pathetic troop of losers, but I really thought you'd do it. After what I told you last night, I just figured..." She shakes her head. "But you didn't do it... I'm sorry if I made you feel bad."

Oh crap. As she hurries away, my instinct is to chase after her and tell her I'm sorry and it was all a misunderstanding. But I can't. Because although I am sorry, I'm also giddy with relief that she was talking about my meeting with Brandon instead of my date with Paige.

And then it occurs to me that even if I had realized she was talking about Brandon, my answers would probably have been the same—because I was too cowardly to leave the group, and I'm still too ashamed to admit it to Abby.

And that doesn't feel so cool.

14

A cell phone goes off at the beginning of lunch break and performs several rounds of the can-can before I realize it's *my* phone. I pull it out, flip open the screen, and check the message: QUAD NOW. BT.

Ordinarily I'd wonder how Brandon got my cell number, or why we'd need another meeting already, but right now I'm far more preoccupied with the prospect of venturing onto the Quad—the centerpiece of Brookbank High. Brandon knows perfectly well that the pristine grassy square is way too important to be sullied by mere students, even though we can view it enviously from most of the corridors. When we arrived at Brookbank we were told that setting foot on the Quad would result in detention, suspension, or whatever punishment Principal Jefferies saw fit to impose. As a result, it has achieved almost mythical status, like the

Hanging Gardens of Babylon, or the grassy knoll. Everyone wants to touch the Quad.

Everyone, that is, except me.

I trudge down the main staircase and peer through the double doors that lead to the Quad. It's already filling up with the imposing physiques of the Ritualites. I swallow hard, push open the door, and shuffle through.

"Mopsely!" yells Brandon, who clearly hasn't picked up on the subtleties of my covert entry. He punches my arm, making perfect contact with the bruise he left there last time.

"Brandon, the, um, Quad. You know, it's—"

"It's fine," says Brandon. "Trust me, everything's cool."

He points to an upper floor window where a group of freshmen boys angles for his attention. I wave at them, and they wave back like they recognize me, or even better, like they think I'm *someone*. Oddly enough it doesn't even surprise me that much anymore.

Truth is, ever since my induction into Brandon's posse I feel like I've been given an unlimited-popularity pass. For years I lived below the poverty line of coolness, in the underworld of geeks and losers. I was tolerated by my fellow dorky cohabitants, but totally dissed by the trendy, beautiful people, who treated me like the excrement sticking to the soles of their personalized designer sneakers. But now the school's royalty pay homage with a discreet nod or grunt, and I can feel my stock rising. The geeks still high-five me because they haven't realized I'm no longer one of them, but that's okay—I'm generous enough to find room for them too.

"Nice to have budding disciples, isn't it?" says Brandon,

pumping his fist in the direction of the freshmen, who seem to have nothing better to do than watch us.

"Yeah," I agree. "It really is."

The friendly chatter around us quiets momentarily, and I turn to see Jefferies standing before us. I duck behind Brandon.

"Gentlemen, I think you know the rules," says Jefferies gruffly.

Brandon steps forward and shakes Jefferies' hand confidently. "Of course, Principal Jefferies. It's just that I felt a meeting to discuss the importance of school pride and history really ought to be conducted in the Quad."

"School pride?"

"Absolutely," says Brandon. "And let's be honest, who epitomizes the Brookbank spirit better than the baseball team, whose successes cast such a positive glow on our beautiful school."

Jefferies nods approvingly. "No one can disagree with that … Well, now, you just keep your meeting orderly and *short*, okay?"

"You have my word," Brandon promises the fast-disappearing Jefferies.

Then Brandon spins around and stares at us, his easygoing demeanor replaced by something rather more disgruntled.

"So you're probably all wondering why I told you to meet here today. Well, it's like I told Jefferies: you need a lesson in school spirit."

He paces back and forth making eye contact with every guy; he'll make a great coach one day.

"To be blunt, Zach says the Strategic Graffiti Campaign isn't going well. Now, I know you're all busy, and I'm willing to cut you some slack for that, but we're a team and we need to work together. I'd like to remind you that when we meet, we're only a small part of something much greater than ourselves. We're continuing traditions that link us to more than four decades of Brookbank seniors. And included in those classes were future politicians, lawyers, and stockbrokers—esteemed men who understood the value of teamwork."

Brandon stops moving and nods paternally at Zach.

"Yeah," grunts Zach, fidgeting like he's afraid of forgetting what he's supposed to say. "So, only a few of the girls' bathroom stalls have been graffitied, and most of it's kind of lame." He looks genuinely disappointed. "I mean, this is pretty simple shit, guys. You check that the restrooms aren't in use, then walk in, pick a stall, and write something crappy about some chick who had it coming. Like, am I the only one here who remembers that time freshman year when Sarah Howard got her first period during Physics and totally freaked out? That's the kind of stuff we've got to come up with. And if you haven't got the balls to write in permanent marker—yeah, I'm talking to you, Caleb—then don't bother doing it at all. It's not funny if they can erase it right away. Got it?"

Everyone nods but the Quad remains silent. I can't tell whether it's because the guys feel chastened or because they're utterly appalled by what they've just heard.

"Um, Zach," I mumble. "Isn't that kind of mean?"

Everyone laughs derisively, but Brandon quiets them with a raised hand.

"No, no. It's a fair question. Look," he says, giving me his undivided attention, "it'd be mean if the girls weren't in on the joke, but they like it too. Seriously, just ask Paige or Morgan or Taylor... any of the hot girls. They think the Rituals are kind of funny."

"Um, okay."

"Good, I'm glad we cleared that up. Now onto the Book of Busts. What's new?"

My hands are trembling as I pull out the book and point to Paige Tramell's senior portrait. Everyone leans forward, squinting to read the numbers.

There's a deathly silence. No one moves. All eyes are trained on the book, and the set of figures beneath the photo.

"Mopsely, you are... THE MAN," yells Brandon, high-fiving me. Actually it's not quite a high-five—more like a creepy Masonic handshake—but I can tell it's a sign of respect.

Just as I feel myself swept along in the excitement, Zach snorts loudly.

"You're kidding, right? 34B? In her dreams, maybe. Paige wouldn't even scrape a 32A without some serious padding." Zach looks up as Brandon shoots him a disapproving stare. "Come on, Brandon. These numbers might work for someone who actually *has* tits, but they sure don't work for Paige."

Brandon scratches his chin thoughtfully. "How did you get these numbers, Kev?"

I close the book and place it gently back in my bag.

"Well, at the date yesterday I did a little behind-the-scenes research."

Zach snorts. "Your research sucks, you loser."

I can feel myself shrinking back against the wall. I'm afraid that Zach is going to ask me to describe my research, and I'm not sure my answer will impress anyone. But then, to my surprise, Brandon intervenes:

"Hey, Zach, at least he's out there doing something, taking one for the team. I don't see you doing much."

Zach looks mortified. "Come on, Brandon. How can you let him compile the book when he thinks Paige scores a 34B? With the right surgery she might make it, but for now her tits are smaller than your pecs."

Brandon clearly appreciates the comparison.

"Then let's edit the numbers," I say, hurriedly redirecting the conversation. "There's no reason why other people can't have input. I say 34B, Zach says 32A, so let's settle on 32B, okay?"

I don't suppose for a moment that it'll fly, but then Brandon slaps me on the back and says yeah, and just like that the matter is settled.

"You're kidding," Zach fumes, his jaw muscles flexing. "This is a joke, Brandon. He's screwing up the book—"

"Lighten up, Zach." Brandon rolls his eyes. "God, you're getting to be a real bore. I guess Taylor's holding out on you these days, huh?"

Zach is about to say something when Brandon flips him the bird. And just like that the discussion is over.

"All right, guys, that'll do it for now," says Brandon.

"But before you go, make sure you see Ryan. He's got your fake IDs."

A cheer fills the Quad. Everyone pumps fists and bumps chests even more than usual. I keep a safe distance.

"Why do we need fake IDs?" I ask.

The cheering ceases. Fists stop mid-pump.

"He's got to go, Brandon," Zach says through clenched teeth. "The guy's a total dork."

"He's just kidding, Zach." Brandon looks at me, adding expectantly, "Unless he has another way to get hold of booze for prom."

"Um, not exactly." I swallow hard. "But what if we get caught?"

"See what I mean?" groans Zach. "He's got no clue."

Brandon just laughs. "Don't be stupid, Zach. He's kidding again. Aren't you, Kevin?"

I sense this is a rhetorical question. "Um, yeah. Yeah, of course."

Everyone else laughs too, and Brandon rewards me by ruffling my hair.

"God, Kev, you're so funny. Everyone always fixated on your dorkiness, but no one ever mentioned how witty you are. It's good to have you on board."

I summon an aw-shucks grin for Brandon, then struggle to hide my amazement as Ryan hands me a fake photo ID. It's more realistic than any of my actual IDs, even though I'm apparently twenty-three years old.

"Do you really think anyone's going to fall for this?" I say, but when I look up, Brandon and Ryan have already taken off.

Suddenly a hand clamps onto my shoulder, rooting me to the spot.

"Almost certainly not," sneers Zach, clearly delighted at this opportunity to inflict discomfort.

I study his face, which isn't difficult as it's only about four inches from mine. He's smiling broadly, but he couldn't appear any more menacing if he pulled a knife.

"Um, hello, Zach."

"The book is a great responsibility, Mopsely."

"Okay."

"And it was supposed to be *my* responsibility."

"Um ... okay."

"I just want you to know I'm onto you, got it? You may be Brandon's best buddy right now, but you're still just a charity case."

"Ok—" I replay that last sentence. "Wait. Did you just say I'm Brandon's best buddy?"

"I wouldn't get too excited," he snarls. "What Brandon gives, Brandon can take away."

Zach administers an unfriendly right jab to my chest and lumbers off with the grace of a heavyweight boxer, but I barely notice. As long as I'm Brandon's best friend, I'm untouchable.

15

English class is eerily empty, like a plague just wiped out half the female contingent. At first I can't think where they've gone, but then I remember, and it totally freaks me out to know that somewhere in the school my mom is teaching girls to avoid boys like Brandon. And me, I guess.

I wait for Paige to appear, and when she finally does I pat the seat beside me so she'll come over, but instead she rushes to the back corner of the room. I wave, but she just buries her head in her *People* magazine and turns bright red. Something about her body language makes me think we may not be repeating our date.

I'm about to turn back to face the front of the class when I'm joined by Jessica Pantley, the ditziest member of the cheerleading squad. She studies me for a moment, then unpacks a pink notebook adorned with flowers and proceeds to write down her observations: "cute dimples, honest face, minimal acne."

"I can see what you're writing, you know," I say.

Jessica lifts a finger to her lips to shush me, then narrows her eyes. She looks uncomfortable, as if the exertion of concentrating is overwhelming. She takes a deep breath and writes: "thoughtful, disarming."

Until recently, I would have thought that seeing my character dissected in Jessica's pink flowery notebook is one of the oddest things that could happen to me in English class. But that was before I began to attract companions like Taylor and Morgan and Paige.

"You'd like to know what I'm doing, wouldn't you?" says Jessica in a high, singsong voice.

"I must admit, I'm slightly confused, yeah."

"It's what I always do before I go on a date with a boy. I study his face and make some notes. That way I can decide if he's someone I'd like to be with."

It's tempting to imagine that I've misunderstood her. But as she gazes at me with enormously wide blue eyes, the thought of being her boyfriend is actually quite appealing.

And then I remember Paige—

"I was sorry to hear about you and Paige," she says, as though all that gazing doubles as mind reading.

"What are you sorry about?"

"Oh, about you two not working out. Paige sounded absolutely brokenhearted, but I think she'll get over it eventually."

I look over my shoulder at Paige, who ducks beneath her *People*.

"I didn't even know we'd stopped—" I begin. But then

I realize that will make me sound like a complete loser. "I guess we're just not meant to be together, you know?"

Jessica nods sympathetically and takes my hand between hers, holding me in the spell of her unwavering gaze.

"Maybe you were meant to break up for a reason," she suggests.

"What reason?"

"Well … so that we could go out."

Even though I'm transfixed by Jessica, I can feel Paige's presence ten feet behind me. It would be so wrong to agree to a date with Jessica less than a day after dating Paige. That would make me the worst kind of player.

"I was thinking tomorrow, after school," she says.

God, she has beautiful eyes.

"If the weather's nice we could go to Brookbank lake."

Blue flecked with green. Aquamarine eyes. Turquoise eyes.

"So what do you think?"

"I'd like that very much," I tell her.

Jessica smiles and nods energetically, then places her hand on my leg.

English is definitely my favorite class.

As soon as I get home, I pull up Google and begin a new search: *breast measurements examples with images*. I've always heard people say that a picture is worth a thousand words, and some pictures are worth even more than that.

The screen fills with links to breast measurements, and

images, and tips for augmentation/reduction, and all I can think is how I've been misusing the Internet until this moment. Clearly the Web was created so that I can have information like this at my fingertips. From now on I'll treat technology with appropriate reverence.

I trawl through images of double-A cup, double-D cup, and everything in-between. There are pictures of different breast types—pert, pendulous—and detailed instructions on how to calculate your bra size. There are even warnings about the dangers of silicone implants, although the images are kind of gross so I go back to admiring the other ones.

After fifteen minutes, I've learned enough to know that Zach may have been on to something when he said Paige is barely a 32A. I close the screen, and I'm about to get up when Mom walks in and sits on the sofa beside the desk. I'm glad she didn't come in a minute sooner.

"So how was the date last night? Now that Abby's not here, you can actually try being honest."

"It was good. I had fun."

"So you're going out again?"

Uh-oh. I really don't want to admit that I'm going on a date with a different girl so soon. Then again—

"Yeah, I'm going on another date tomorrow," I say, hoping she'll assume it's with Paige.

"Oh, that's nice. You must have made a connection then." She hesitates a moment, then stands up.

I'm so pleased she misunderstood me that I conjure a broad smile, and she smiles back. But somehow her smile seems empty, like I've just told her the very thing she didn't want to hear.

16

She's so notoriously ditzy that I half-expect Jessica to forget our date by the time school ends the next day, but I spend the final period chewing gum just in case. The image of Paige's face as I ate the chips and salsa is still branded on my memory, and I don't want there to be any obstacles to full-on French kissing this time.

I walk out of school and there's Jessica, waiting by the main doors just like we arranged. Well, not exactly like we arranged—she's kneeling in the grass, winding daisies into a chain. When she sees me she waves, and a moment later she's wearing the daisy chain around her head and I'm wondering if this date is such a good idea after all.

Not that she isn't cute. She's wearing a figure-hugging, sky blue tube dress that ends a gratifyingly long way above her knees, and her legs are tan like she spends most of her life outdoors making daisy chains. She reminds me of a character from one of those age-swapping movies; it'd sure be easier to explain her behavior if she were actually an eight-year-old trapped in an eighteen-year-old's body, even though that would make this date kind of immoral.

"Take my car?" she asks, skipping over to me.

"Uh, sure."

"Or we could take yours," she adds thoughtfully.

"No, I don't have a car."

"Oh." Her eyes grow wide and she bites a fingernail. "You probably shouldn't admit that. It's not cool."

"Okay. How about we pretend I have a car but we'd prefer to take yours?"

"That'd work. Although it's actually my sister's car."

"Isn't it uncool to admit that?" I say as we traipse across the grass toward the student parking lot.

"No, 'cause I'm a girl. And 'cause I have access to a convertible Beetle. That makes it okay."

Her logic temporarily eludes me, but rumor has it that extended questioning rarely leads to clarification when it comes to Jessica, so I let it go. And then she's opening the doors to a shiny new Bug, and I think she may be right about this being the next best thing to owning your own car.

"I'm going to open the roof, okay?" she giggles, pulling back the black canvas top. She's finished before I have a chance to answer.

A few minutes later we're whistling along residential streets and Jessica, minus daisy chain, is trying to coax her hair up so that it will fly around in the breeze. She seems unsure that it's working and spends most of the time checking her reflection in the rearview mirror.

"Don't you just love to feel the wind in your hair?" she bubbles. "It's so liberating."

"I don't have much hair."

"Oh, then you should get a wig or something. No one should miss out on this."

Once again the tiny, rational part of my brain wants to ask her how on earth I could feel a wig, but this is Jessica, and so the best course of action is to pretend we're having parallel, unrelated conversations.

"So where are we going?" I ask, as the buildings begin to thin out.

"I think you'd look good with long blond hair," she gushes. "It'd look kind of feminine, but I think I'd like that."

"Are we going far?"

"Although blond might not work with your pasty complexion."

"Do you like spring? I like the warmer weather."

"Maybe long brown hair. I could braid it for you."

"Long hair wouldn't be so good when the weather gets warmer."

"I like the warmer weather. Do you like spring?"

I take a deep breath and marvel at this unlikely confluence of conversations. "Yeah, I like spring."

"Hmmm, interesting," she sighs, then shuts up completely. Strangely, this is an improvement.

Five minutes later she pulls into the parking lot beside Brookbank lake. She looks around nervously, gets out, and walks swiftly toward a secluded clump of trees. When we're past the first tree she grabs my hand and performs a couple of pirouettes beneath my outstretched arm.

"I like you, Kevin. I think you're funny."

"Um, thank you. I think."

"Do you think it's a compliment to be called funny?" she asks with sudden deathly seriousness.

"Er … I'm not sure, really. I guess not."

"What about hunk? Would it be a compliment to call you a hunk?"

"Well, yeah, although we'd both know it's not true."

Jessica is sweeping her foot across the ground, brushing the grass back and forth. "Hmmm. So what compliment *would* you like to hear?"

I expect to see her laughing at me, but she's actually serious. I'm beginning to reflect nostalgically on our conversation in the car.

"I don't know. Maybe interesting. Or genuine."

Her eyes open wide and her mouth contorts. "That's *it*? Interesting or genuine? Geez, you aim pretty low. I thought you'd at least try for good kisser." She looks away coyly. "Are you?"

"Am I what?"

"A good kisser." She takes my hand and performs another pirouette.

I turn a deep shade of red. "Not really," I mumble.

We disconnect and she plants her hands on her hips. "Ooooh, that's not a good way to put it. Way too honest. Try again."

"Um … I … yes, I'm amazing."

"Naaaah. Wrong answer. Kind of gross. Try again."

"Geez, why can't I just show you?"

"Ah," she whispers. "Definitely getting warmer."

And then she's holding my hand again and our lips are touching, and I'm content to stay that way as long as she likes. I don't change a thing about our gentle, moist little kisses until she opens her mouth, and then I do exactly what Paige told me to do. And it works. Jessica doesn't pull away for at least ten seconds.

"Whoa, you actually *are* a good kisser."

"Thanks," I say, preparing to continue.

She leans back. "But your hard-on is rubbing against me and it's weirding me out."

Why do guys have such an overtly expressive sexual organ?

"But don't worry," she reassures me. "It's just a little time-out, that's all." She smiles and takes my hand. "Do you think I'm cute?"

I look away. "Yes."

"I'm glad." She chuckles. "Ever since that Women's Studies class started, some of the girls are saying you shouldn't judge someone on their looks. But I don't see what's so wrong with being pretty."

"No. I like pretty girls."

She raises an eyebrow. "Ooooh, that sounded kind of weird."

"Sorry. I didn't mean—"

"Forget about it ... I'm just saying it's not fair for someone to hate me just because I've got the same physical measurements as Jessica Alba, you know?"

"Hold on. Did you just say Jessica Alba?"

"Yeah. Isn't that incredible?"

Yup, that is incredible.

"That's exactly what Paige said."

"She did?" Jessica furrows her eyebrows and stares into space. "Oh, it must have been Paris Hilton then, not Jessica Alba." She gazes at me again. "Sorry, I didn't mean to remind you about your ex-girlfriend."

Ex-girlfriend? My date with Paige only lasted seventeen minutes. Is it really possible to become an item in less time than it takes to shower?

"Well, anyway," continues Jessica proudly, "I just got measured for my prom dress. And it turns out I'm a 34B-25-35. Do you need me to repeat that?"

"Huh? No, I got it." I give her breasts a closer inspection. "Are you really a 34B?"

"Yeah, of course. Why would I lie about something like that?" She pauses as I shrug. "Here, you can touch if you want."

I wait a moment, expecting her to say "April Fools'" even though it's almost May, but she doesn't say a word, and she's moving toward me. I swallow hard, then place my hands on her breasts and give a little push.

"Ow!" She steps back. "Geez, Kevin. It's best if you touch a girl's breasts gently. They're kind of sensitive, in case you hadn't heard."

Actually, I hadn't heard, but I don't tell her that.

"Try it like this," she says, gently rubbing her fingertips across the part where I imagine the nipples must be.

I take over and she smiles, and I know that I'm doing well. I'm even considerately keeping my distance so that my boner doesn't disturb her again. I begin to entertain visions of a long and enjoyable evening.

"Good, you've got it." She removes my hands. "So, you believe me now?"

"About what?"

"They're 34B, right? It's obvious."

"Oh yeah. 34B. Absolutely."

"Great. Well, this was nice."

She does one final pirouette and wanders out of the woods.

I'm trying to keep up with what just happened. It seemed like we'd made a real connection. But I don't want to sound desperate—even though I am—so I just trot along behind her.

As she gets into the car I notice a bumper sticker emblazoned against the Beetle's red paint: *I have PMS and a handgun. Any questions?*

"Is that bumper sticker true?"

Jessica puts the keys in the ignition. "Which part?"

"Um, the bit about you having a gun."

She laughs. "Is that what scares you the most?"

"Yeah, of course."

She laughs again. "Then you don't know girls at all, Mr. Mopsely." She's facing the passenger seat as if I were already sitting next to her. "That's really an elementary—"

I don't hear what comes after that because she's driven off without me, although she continues talking to the invisible Kevin Mopsely all the way out of the parking lot.

In the hour it takes me to walk home, I wonder how long our conversation lasted before she noticed I wasn't even there.

17

It's been two months since I've seen my dad, although he only lives twelve miles away. Like most realtors, he shows open houses on the weekends, and I can't say I've felt much of an urge to see him, anyway. Until now, that is.

Over the last two weeks my life has taken several strange turns for the better, but I can't share the good news with the two people I talk to the most: Mom and Abby. They'd both freak out and they'd both hate me and I'd still have to face them every day. This is just the kind of situation where absent, adulterous fathers come in handy.

He's supposed to pick me up at lunchtime, but lunchtime comes and goes and we don't hear from him. Mom pretends that nothing is out of the ordinary because she tries not to badmouth Dad to my face, but by four o'clock I call his cell phone to tell him that she's dropping me off at his house. He doesn't answer, which means he's ignoring me because he always keeps his cell phone on. I leave a message telling him I'll be there in half an hour.

I know it kills Mom to have to drive me over to his new home. It's actually his girlfriend's house, but by the time he admitted to his extracurricular activities, he'd pretty much moved in there already. It's in a new, suburban gated community for middle-class people who believe that everyone's out to get them. Dad must feel quite at home.

When we pull up to the gates, I'm surprised to see that he's already waiting for me. He waves halfheartedly and wanders over to our car. Mom gets out before I can stop her.

"Hey, Kevin," says Dad. "We'll be heading right out, okay? Things to see, people to do, you know." He laughs at his own wit. "Hello, Maggie."

He swoops in to peck Mom on the cheek, but as he does she sniffs the air suspiciously.

"Have you been drinking, Darrell?"

Dad rolls his eyes. "Just drop it, okay?"

"No, I won't drop it. You know I don't like you driving when you've been drinking."

"It's just one drink—"

They continue to bicker, but I've already heard enough, so I pick up my bag and let myself into the passenger side of Dad's car. Mom doesn't realize what I've done, but Dad notices and as soon as I'm inside he waves goodbye and hustles over to join me. Before Mom can protest further, we're pulling out into traffic.

"Christ, that was annoying." Dad slaps the steering wheel for effect.

"Well, we haven't had many of these family reunions yet. Maybe it'll get easier over time."

"Yeah, sure," he snorts. "And maybe she'll buy herself some clothes that actually look decent, and dye her hair like every other woman."

I laugh in spite of myself. I suppose I'd never realized that Mom's appearance bugged him too.

Dad notices me laughing and looks over. He has a wicked grin on his face. "See, we both know some things'll never change."

"I guess not."

"I know not."

Dad looks different than I remember. He's dyed his hair black, and there seems to be more of it than before. He's even wearing a new tan leather jacket, which makes him look trendier, more youthful. I'm glad that at least one of my parents is taking care of themselves.

We pull into an ugly, concrete apartment complex, where an ostentatiously large sign proudly proclaims that these are The Grovington Apartments. A part of me wants to know what we're doing here, but another part of me certainly doesn't, so I remain mute and follow him out of the car. Dad steps up to the nearest first-floor apartment and unlocks the door with one of the keys on his chain. He walks in and beckons me to follow.

"Ta-da!" he booms, as though I'm supposed to be impressed by the stained, cream-colored walls and the worn sofa facing an ancient TV propped up on a beer crate.

"Um, what's going on, Dad?"

Dad shoots me a confused look. "It's my new place," he explains with exaggerated enthusiasm.

"But Mom took me to your new place...that gated community."

Dad shakes his head and smiles. "No. Things didn't work out with Kimberly, see?"

I'm trying to process this, but it requires some serious work. He left his wife of twenty-two years for this woman, and now, barely eight months later, he acts like it's no big deal that it didn't work out.

Dad pulls a couple cans of beer from a crate beside the sofa and hands one to me. I wait for him to take it back, say he's kidding, but he's already focused on his own. I hold the can tightly in both hands—it's warm, but it's beer so I'll drink it anyway.

"Does it bother you that things didn't work out?" I ask finally.

"Not really, no." He forces a laugh. "Kimberly was a total bitch."

I try to hide my shock, but "bitch" certainly wasn't part of Dad's vocabulary when he lived with us. Seems as though his drastic makeover wasn't limited to clothes and hair.

"So . . . well, what happened?"

"I'll tell you what happened," he mutters. "I mistook Kimberly for a smart woman—someone who'd let me be myself, without judging me the whole time. Stupid, aren't I? First your mom, then her. I'm batting 0-for-two. Not a good average."

"So what's next?"

He swigs his beer and frowns. "Well, for one thing, I'm

not going to get trapped again. See, I realize now that women are all about trapping guys. They talk about lack of commitment and stuff like that as if it's some big character flaw, and so you feel all guilty and before you know it—BAM, you're engaged, or married, and it's all over."

He chugs the whole beer and so I chug mine as well. Immediately my body erupts in a belch and tears sting my eyes. Dad barely seems to notice as he pulls out two more.

"See," he continues earnestly, "there's nothing wrong with being in a relationship *per se*, but you've got to stay on at least even terms, know what I mean? Like, if you want to have some girl, then have her."

"I do," I tell him, although it feels like it's someone else saying it; the beer is already working its magic. "Twice this week I had dates with different girls."

Dad raises his beer and knocks it against mine as a kind of masculine toast to my burgeoning libido. "That's excellent, son. What're they like?"

"Well, Paige is hot as hell, and Jessica's kind of ditzy but she's cute as well. Come to think of it, they're both really sexy."

I can't believe I'm actually saying these things, but it feels good to open up at last, and I couldn't ask for a more appreciative audience.

"So if this Paige girl is so hot, why'd you want to go out with Jessica?"

Hmmm, tricky one that, since I'm not exactly sure myself what happened there.

"I guess I didn't want to get pinned down by her," I say, improvising. "Although I must admit that I did feel kind of bad going out with Jessica so soon afterwards. And I didn't have the guts to tell Paige that it was all over."

"Hey, forget the guilt, okay?" Dad's wagging his finger at me and looking stern. "It's not like they wouldn't put one over on you if they could. You know it."

"Um, maybe."

"Yeah, so …" Dad polishes off another beer but this time I don't think I can keep up with him. "So Paige wasn't exactly Little Miss Perfect, huh?"

"No. She's kind of vapid and self-obsessed—"

"Oh, you've got to watch the self-obsessed ones. They're the worst. One moment all you can think about is how hot they are, the next you're wondering why they completely rule your life. Take my advice—get whatever you want from whoever you want, then move on."

"But isn't that kind of cruel?"

He's wagging his finger again. "Forget cruel. I played the part of dutiful husband for two decades, and let me tell you something, they don't hand out any medals." He shakes his head. "No sir, they weren't lying when they said that nice guys finish last. So I say, stop trying. Just accept that it's in a man's nature to sow his oats."

What has this man done with my father?

"Look," he continues, gaining momentum with every sip of beer, "I've been reading this book that proves how men are genetically programmed to seek multiple partners; it's all about evolution and survival of the fittest. So it's really not our fault, 'cause it's just in our nature to play the field. To deny that is to deny what makes us human." He takes a deep breath and sighs. "You wouldn't want to deny what makes you a man, would you, Kevin?"

I hesitate. So much of what he's saying is confusing, if not downright freaky, but I can't deny that it's reassuring to have my own experiences rationalized and justified.

"No, Dad. I wouldn't want that."

The corner of Dad's mouth twists into a wry smile. "You're a good kid, Kevin. I know I can trust you not to make the same mistakes I made."

"Um, thanks."

He nods vigorously, like he's proud of me, like I impress him. And I'd be lying if I said it didn't feel wonderfully empowering.

I smile right back.

18

Over the next hour I consume my second and third beers, and discuss my conquests in greater detail. Dad is actively engaged the whole time, encouraging me to realize that the only thing I did wrong was to settle for kissing and a grope when I could probably have haggled for more. I'm not sure about that, but he seems absolutely positive, so I promise to move faster and more decisively the next time.

I'm about to ask him for some advice about sex when he leaps up from the sofa and says it's time to head out for dinner. I suggest we stay in so that we can continue talking, but he just laughs and points to the kitchenette, which looks like it hasn't been used in years.

As we head outside, I can feel the beer dulling my senses, slowing my reactions. I have that blurry feeling of my legs being disconnected from the rest of me, although they carry me forward in roughly the right direction.

Then something kicks in—maybe a sixth sense. In any case, it warns me that we shouldn't be getting into Dad's car.

"Um, Dad? I don't think we should be driving."

"Don't be stupid. Get in."

"Seriously, I don't think you're legal."

Dad looks off into the distance and shakes his head. "Not you too. I figured it was just your mom, but I guess you're going to act like her, huh?"

"No, no." Before I know it, I'm fumbling for the seat belt, hoping he can see more clearly than I can.

Dad seems to drive okay, although I'm hardly a reliable judge of what counts as straight. Three beers really shouldn't have this much effect on a person.

I want to ask him what's for dinner but I'm having trouble forming words, so I just sit back and close my eyes and dream of making out with Paige, or Jessica, or Paige *and* Jessica—

"Are you coming or not?" Dad shouts from just outside the passenger's side window.

I hadn't even noticed that we'd stopped moving, but I pull myself out of the seat and stumble across the parking lot to the restaurant entrance. We walk inside and a cute woman with bleach-blond hair says, "Oh hello, Darrell. Your normal table?" and Dad says, "Yeah, Daisy," and then I notice that her enormous boobs are barely contained by her cheerful Hooters top, but something tells me not to mention this to her.

"Damn, Daisy, that top ain't gonna hold 'em in if they get any bigger," Dad says.

Daisy smiles wanly and deposits us at our table before striding away.

"Why are we at Hooters, Dad?"

Dad narrows his eyes like he's examining an alien life form, then points to a sample of the waitresses sauntering around the room.

"Use your eyes, son. This is the kind of view eyes were made for."

I look around, but all I see is a collection of Daisy-clones—phenomenally well-endowed women with fixed smiles and tight shorts.

A waitress makes eye contact with me to indicate that she'll be right over. Moments later she scuttles to my side.

Then she sees Dad.

"Oh, it's you, Darrell," she says like she's just lost a game of spin the bottle. "Would you like your usual?"

"I would, thank you, Amber. But my ... brother might like to order as well."

I can't believe he just said that, and neither can Amber. She rolls her eyes. I can tell she can't wait to leave our table.

"And you'd better bring us a couple of beers each," says Dad.

"Fine, but I'll need to see some ID for your ... brother."

"That's okay," I say. "I don't want any."

I order a burger and fries and spend the next twenty minutes listening to my father identify each of the waitresses. I get the feeling they know he's watching them, because they all cast disgusted looks in our direction and move quickly out of sight. As each one disappears, Dad asks me if I can guess their bra size, and even though I can I don't want him to know it, so instead I listen to him talking me through each answer like it's a math problem that requires serious consideration.

Unfortunately the beers arrive before the food, and Dad digs in. He gets louder as he knocks them back, and his bust-estimates become public knowledge. When Amber finally brings the food he never takes his eyes off her breasts, directing his thanks to the left breast and his request for more beer to the right. The moment he stops talking, she seizes the opportunity to leave.

"D'ya see how she completely shoved them in my face?" he says, his speech slurred.

I don't know what to say, so I stuff my mouth with fries and shrug.

"Yeah, I think she wants me," he confides in a voice that easily carries across the room.

Some guys at the next table laugh loudly, but Dad seems oblivious. The effects of the beer are wearing off me now, and as things come into focus I can't help feeling a little embarrassed to be here with him.

"You don't really believe that waitress finds you attractive, do you?" I ask, hoping that this display is all part of some elaborate self-effacing joke.

"What are you talking about? Every time I come here she remembers my name. And you've seen the way she stands right next to our table."

"'Cause she's a waitress. And she probably remembers your name because you tip well, or because she thinks you're old and fatherly."

Dad wields a chicken wing menacingly. "That's got

nothing to do with it. She thinks I'm good-looking, and she doesn't know I'm older than her, so don't go blowing it for me."

I almost choke on my burger. "What... you're not thinking of asking her out on a date or anything, are you?"

"Yeah, of course I am. That's why we're here. Talking to you this evening finally made me realize that I've got to seize the bull by the horns, and there's no time like the present, and all that crap."

"But... but..." I gasp, struggling for words. I feel suddenly sober, like someone's doused me with ice water. I know that I can't let him ask her out or she'll probably have him arrested for stalking, or indecency, or being inappropriately old. But what can I do? I try to concentrate, and all the while Dad chugs beer, his movements cumbersome and his voice booming. I have the feeling all eyes in the room are on us, even though I can't bear to look around and check.

"Next time Amber comes by, I'll ask her," he says, clearly delighted with this foolproof plan. "I bet it'll make her night."

I twist around to look for her, but she's nowhere to be seen. I have to prevent this from happening. I know I do. I'd die from embarrassment, and I'm not sure I'd ever be able to speak to my father again.

"Can we go, please?"

"Don't be stupid. I'm waiting for Amber."

Okay, so Plan A just failed. Time for Plan B.

"I'm just going to the bathroom," I say.

As Dad washes down another chicken wing with his beer, I hurry over to the hostess' desk at the entrance. Daisy is still there, but she doesn't seem thrilled to see me. I guess it's guilt by association.

"Um, I know this is weird," I stammer, "but I really need to get us out of here right now."

Daisy tilts her head and puts her hands on her hips. "And I'm supposed to care?"

"No, I guess not. What do I need to do to make sure Amber doesn't come back to our table?"

"Hmmm," she muses, leaning against her desk. "Well, you could just settle the bill."

Before she can say another word, I pull out the emergency credit card Mom gave me, and Daisy disappears with it. A minute later she reappears with a credit slip for sixty dollars and suggests that a generous tip really helps the waitresses look charitably on some of their more "deplorable" customers. She says it just like that, and I'm surprised to hear a busty woman with bleach-blond hair use such big words. But then I imagine what Mom would say to me if she knew I'd thought such a thing, so I add a twenty dollar tip and hightail it back to the table.

Dad's looking around the room vacantly, wondering where his beloved waitress has gone. His beer bottles are empty, but I don't think he needs any more—he looks like he's about to pass out.

I wrap an arm around him and drag him across the restaurant, to the amusement of the other diners. All the way, he keeps protesting that Amber will be over soon and he needs to speak to her. A couple of the neighboring tables cheer as we leave; when even Hooters patrons recognize how profoundly desperate Dad sounds, I know things are grim.

We step outside, and the cool air feels refreshing. Dad reaches for his car keys, but there's no way I'm letting him drive. I don't know the way to his apartment, so I hail a taxi that's hovering nearby. The driver pulls up and I open the door for Dad, who crashes in.

"I ain't taking no drunk dude," the driver says. "I'd need an extra ten bucks to take him."

I say that'll be fine, and I tell him the Grovington Apartments, and he looks at me like I must be kidding. Dad mumbles the address, then loses consciousness.

The driver pulls up at the apartment and I hand him the credit card, and he informs me that there's a five dollar surcharge for credit cards. It bugs me, although I guess I should be grateful he only asked for five. I'd have paid twenty if that's what it took.

I take Dad's keys and open the door. The apartment looks even more squalid than it did earlier.

"Where's the spare bed, Dad?"

He points to the sofa and chuckles. I pull it out and notice it still has dirty sheets on it.

"Where are you sleeping?" I say.

Dad points to the sofa bed because it's the only bed in the apartment.

Ten minutes later we're lying side by side, and his snoring is making the walls shake.

When I wake up the next day, Dad's already left to do an open house. A spare key is taped to the TV along with a note saying there's a coffee shop down the street where I can get breakfast. He'll be home around five, it says.

I'm tempted to call Mom for a ride home so I can spend the day doing something enjoyable, but I know I shouldn't—one glance at Dad's squalid apartment and she'd be moved to stage an intervention. Besides, the way Dad's been behaving this weekend, I don't think her help would be appreciated. So I find the coffee shop, then go to a second-run movie theater next door, and finally hang out in a book store.

At five o'clock I'm back at the apartment, but Dad's not there. I watch the Discovery Channel for another couple hours, but he still doesn't show. Finally, I call Mom to come and pick me up, only I don't really know where I am so it's hard to give directions.

At eight o'clock she knocks on the door. I turn the lights out so she can't see inside, and we walk to the car in silence. We don't talk all the way home, because she doesn't want to criticize Dad and I don't want to relive the weekend.

But I must admit that it wasn't a complete waste of time, because I've learned a valuable lesson: lusting after sexy girls is only cool when you're young.

Which is why I'd better enjoy it while I can.

19

I wake up with a panic attack the next morning because there just aren't enough days left in the school year. Under any other circumstances this would be a sign of grave illness, possibly of impending insanity. But I know I'm not insane, because things are different now. I've had two dates in the past week. Before that, I had zero dates in eighteen years. Even though math has never been my best subject, in my feverish state I do the following calculation and it makes me realize that time is short:

2 dates per wk x 2.5 wks remaining until prom
= 5 pre-prom dates

I resolve to make the most of every remaining day. But then I do another, hypothetical calculation and it makes me wish I were still a junior:

$$2 \text{ dates per wk} \times 54.5 \text{ wks until prom}$$
$$= 109 \text{ pre-prom dates}$$

Yes, 109 dates. All with different girls. Now, it's true that there aren't 109 girls in my class I would actually want to date—or even 109 girls, come to think of it—but that's not the point. It's the thought that, had things been different, I'd be the kind of guy who lines up 109 dates in little more than a year. But instead, the vagaries of the academic calendar are robbing me of this opportunity. And it doesn't seem fair.

I fume about this all the way to school, but by lunchtime I've set up a date on Wednesday with Kayla Reid, so I begin to feel better about things. One pre-prom date down, four to go.

And then Taylor Carson asks for a date the same evening, and because she's hot I get flustered and say yes, and suddenly my concerns are altogether different.

I start by trying to put off Kayla, because she's not as cute as Taylor. She's taller than me, has significantly more muscular legs, and wears a perpetually bored expression. But she's also got Angelina Jolie's lips, and a tongue-stud that she uses to great effect when making out.

Or so I'm told.

I stop her after school and tell her I can't make it on Wednesday, and she tells me that I *can* make it and I *will* make it.

And I say, "Yes, you're right." Because, like I said, she's bigger and more muscular than me.

On Tuesday, I manage to catch Taylor just as English class is beginning. I say that since she's dating Zach I can't go out with her in good conscience, even though the thought of giving Zach the shaft is positively irresistible. She says they've broken up, so I don't need to worry. I manage to hide my surprise and delight, then ask her if she'd like to try another night instead, because I'm busy on Wednesday. She looks deeply wounded, and asks me if it's because I dislike her or find her unattractive. Even though I know she's a born actress, I'm wracked with guilt. I promise to spend Wednesday with her.

Ms. Kowalski is hovering near my table, eavesdropping on our conversation. I don't get Ms. K. She's lost almost two-thirds of the girls in her class now, yet she's never seemed happier. But every time she sees me she shakes her head and looks away. I'm tempted to turn up to class with a big scarlet *A* painted on my T-shirt, but that might count as being dorky, so I probably shouldn't.

"Still five of you left," she sighs, scanning the faces of the remaining girls disappointedly. "I guess the cheerleading squad just likes my class that much, huh?"

I can't believe it didn't occur to me before now, but all of my dates have been or will be with members of the cheerleading squad: Paige, Jessica, Kayla, Taylor. It's a remarkable coincidence, and I'm fortunate that they're also the girls who have chosen to avoid my mom's class.

Ms. K slumps in her chair, then looks up imploringly. "Why not give Professor Donaldson's class a chance? You might be impressed."

Paige snorts. "I'm pretty comfortable with my femininity, thank you," she says curtly.

"But that's not really the point. Feminism is hardly synonymous with femininity."

"Well, duh! If it was, feminists would be cute and like themselves more."

I half-expect Ms. K to scream at Paige, but instead she just looks tired and sad.

"What about you, Taylor? Do you feel the same way as Paige?"

"Oh geez, I—"

"Of course she does," Paige assures us, casting a level stare at Taylor. "We're in this together."

"In *what?*" moans Ms. K. "What on earth does 'We're in this together' mean?" She returns her attention to Taylor. "I just can't believe you'd feel the same way as Paige. If this is some kind of weird popularity contest, I'd like to point out that most girls have moved on to Professor Donaldson's class, so you're actually in the minority by staying here."

"It's not the *female* majority we're interested in," laughs Paige flirtatiously, kicking back in her chair and smiling confidently as all male eyes focus on her.

I take a moment to look around the room at the other cheerleaders, expecting to see them mirroring Paige's carefree laughter. But they're not smiling. Taylor is studying her pen, Jessica is staring intently out the window, and Morgan is shaking her head like she's just not sure about any of this.

Only I don't know what *this* is. I just know there's a schism forming among the cheerleaders, and Paige seems blissfully unaware of it. She continues to flash her smile at the boys around her. She even throws in a few carefully executed lower lip nibbles to be extra cute.

But it doesn't do anything for me. For the first time, even though I can't quite believe it myself, I don't find her attractive at all.

20

Brandon schedules the next meeting for Wednesday lunchtime, which means I'll have to stand Abby up at lunch again. This will annoy her because she'll know where I am and she won't like it. We've avoided the topic since our run-in last week, but I know it still bugs her. Even the last quartet practice seemed kind of flat.

On the way to the meeting I stop off at the vending machine to grab a can of Dr. Pepper. Almost immediately Brandon sidles up, tutting loudly.

"Not impressive, Kev," he sighs.

"Oh, I don't normally drink this stuff, but—"

"That's not what I mean. I'm talking about the fact that you're about to put money in this machine." He slides in front of me and holds down the Diet 7-Up and Diet Coke buttons. "Now push the button you want," he instructs.

I hesitate a moment, wondering if I'm about to become the butt of a joke. If so, at least there's no one around to see it.

I tentatively push the Dr. Pepper button. A can rolls out. A Dr. Pepper can, to be precise.

"The guy who owns the vending machine compiled the Book of Busts back in 1973," Brandon says, like this explains what just happened. "He's old as hell now, but he still remembers the glory days at Brookbank."

I try to hide my smile. "Did you just get me a free Dr. Pepper?"

"Damn right."

"But how?"

"The owner rewired it for us." Brandon leans over and helps himself to a Mountain Dew. "But only important people know about this trick, so if you tell anyone else, there'll be hell to pay. Understand?"

"Yeah. Course."

"Cool." He cracks open his can and bumps it against mine. "So all you have to do is press the Diet 7-Up and Diet Coke buttons at the same time as the one you actually want. It takes a bit of practice, but you'll get it."

"What if I want Diet 7-Up or Diet Coke?"

Brandon's upper lip curls. "Diet drinks are for girls. You're not a girl, are you?"

"Um, no."

"Good. Then there's no problem, right?"

"Well, no. But doesn't the guy who stocks the machine notice there are cans missing?"

Brandon laughs. "Oh, that's the best thing of all. Because

the inventory never balances out on this machine, the owner can use it as evidence to fire employees who aren't pulling their weight. So we get free drinks and he gets to run a more efficient business."

"But ... that's illegal, isn't it?"

Brandon puts his arm across my shoulders and lowers his voice. "Do you realize how hard it is to fire people legally these days? Even complete slackers are untouchable. I'm telling you, every time we take a can we're making the world a better place."

"Oh."

"And remember what I said about us being part of something bigger than ourselves? This is exactly what I'm talking about. We're like a fraternity, only without the Greek letters—"

"Or the kegs," I remind him.

"Huh? No way. We have the kegs."

"Oh."

Brandon turns and ambles along the corridor. He doesn't seem to mind me tagging along.

"What I'm saying is, back in 1973 this owner guy was *you*, Kev. He was the *man*. And when you're the man, people'll always look out for you." He ruffles my hair. "You do realize you're the man now, right?"

"Um ... yeah, I guess."

"Good. 'Cause there's something I need to give you."

Brandon stops beside his locker and opens it. He reaches in and removes a sturdy black box with the reverence normally reserved for holy relics. Inside the box, layer upon layer of tissue paper covers a cracked, ancient-looking, brown leather book.

"This," whispers Brandon, "is the original Book of Busts."

As he gently places it in my hands, my first thought is that it's about to fall apart. Not only does the cover bring new meaning to the term "distressed leather," but the book is stuffed to bursting with dog-eared pieces of paper in every imaginable shade of yellow, cream, and off-white. Every page chronicles a portion of each senior class of Brookbank girls, and all the pages have been meticulously bound together with string.

I turn to the beginning of the book, where the photographs are pretty faded. I notice that the numbers below the photos haven't changed much over the years, but that's less extraordinary than the horrific array of over-permed and beehive hairstyles; truthfully, having Jessica Alba's figure wouldn't help any of these girls.

I leaf through until I reach the 1980s, figuring there'll be a higher proportion of hotties here, but instead my eyes are assaulted by a criminally large number of wild, gel-induced bangs. It's not until I get to the twenty-first century that I find myself the slightest bit attracted to Brookbank's senior girls.

"Amazing, isn't it," says Brandon. "It's a historical document, when you think about it."

"It's old, all right."

"And now it's yours to keep until you've completed the entries for our year. When you're done, we'll remove the sheets from your folder and bind them into the book." He nods his head approvingly. "You've earned this, Kev. You're really getting the job done. I'm proud of you."

"Um, thanks, Brandon. I appreciate you saying that." I feel a little choked up. "Look, I just have to ask…why me? I mean, this is such an honor, and I guess I still don't get why you let me do it."

"Can you imagine any of the other guys appreciating the significance of an antique like this?" he laughs.

I laugh too. "I guess not."

Brandon looks up and down the corridor, and thinks for a moment. "Okay, look, it's true that the head of the Rituals usually keeps the book for himself, or gives it to one of the most popular guys in school as a reward. But the way I see it, all that does is limit the Rituals to a small group."

Brandon closes his locker and gazes longingly at the book, like he isn't quite ready to bid it farewell.

"Back when it started, the Book of Busts involved *everybody*. It was a source of school pride. But over the years, the other parts of the Graduation Rituals—the Alternative Yearbook, the Strategic Graffiti Campaign—got added, and the significance of the book got diluted. Now most guys don't even bother to join in at all. So when you said you wanted to do the book, I realized this was my chance to remind everyone that the Rituals are bigger than any one person."

"That's for sure."

"And look at you now. You're popular, and unlike most of the other guys you deserve that, because you've taken your job seriously. And future generations of Brookbank seniors are going to remember you for it too."

I have to admit that his hyperbole is quite alluring. "You really think so?"

"Absolutely. You're the guy who's going to prove that the book is still relevant … You're my legacy, Kev. I know you won't let me down."

Once the meeting begins, Brandon turns to Spud and wrings his hands anxiously, which is an unusual sight.

"So Spud, about the Alternative Yearbook … "

Spud nods.

"Well, we, like, put you in charge of it … "

Spud nods.

"And, like, from what I've been hearing you haven't exactly been asking around for information … or help."

Spud nods.

"So I guess what I'm saying is, are you into the whole Alternative Yearbook thing?"

Spud nods. "Dude."

Brandon visibly relaxes. "Cool. So you're making progress?"

Spud nods. "Dude."

"So can we see what you've got so far?"

"Whoa," grunts Spud, like a pit bull guarding a bone.

Brandon drops the matter because he values his life. Then he looks over my way and asks for an update. I notice he doesn't seem as intimidated by me.

"Well," I say, leaning back in my chair, "I've got an entry for Jessica Pantley."

"Cool. Who gave you that?"

"No one. I got it myself."

"So ... you had a date with Jess Pantley?"

"Yup."

At least half the jaws in the room are hanging open, and although it's not a pretty sight, the effect is quite empowering.

Brandon tries to hide his surprise. "So what are her stats?"

I pretend to study the book as if I haven't actually memorized them already. "34B-25-35."

"34B my ass," shouts Zach. "Don't tell me, you used the same scientific guesswork as before."

"Actually, I felt them, and they're right on 34B."

"You felt them? Or did you just have a grope while she was still wearing a bra?"

I don't say anything.

"See! You didn't touch them at all. She was probably wearing a padded bra, you moron." He looks imploringly at Brandon. "Come on, Brandon, it's time for dorkus here to go."

"Zach," says Brandon soothingly, "the fact is, Kev has filled in the blanks under two prized girls, in one week. All you had to do was dish the dirt on Taylor—who happens to be your girlfriend, by the way—but you haven't even managed that. So until you can prove to us that you're worthy of the job, how about you get off Kevin's case?"

Being Brandon's best buddy has some real perks.

Zach nods slowly. "All right, I'll get you Taylor's numbers," he mumbles. "Leave it to me."

A part of me wants to say that this is quite unlikely since

she's dumped him. But then I wonder, what if she hasn't actually dumped him? What if she's just two-timing him? And so I decide to keep my mouth shut.

But I'll still go on a date with her, because if she is two-timing Zach, I'll enjoy myself even more.

21

It's getting easy to tell Mom I'll be home late. She persists in the quaint, old-fashioned notion that every time I announce I'm going out on a date it will be with the same person as before, so I let her believe it. It's not even lying.

Kayla texts me to say that we'll be going to a movie at 7:30, and I immediately text Taylor to say we'll meet at the same theater at 9:30. Then I brush my teeth and floss and put on a J. Crew shirt that Abby says looks really good on me.

I take one last look in the mirror and tell myself that it's going to be fine. All I have to do is make sure the movie we choose is less than two hours long, and lose Kayla as soon as it ends. Yeah, it'll be fine.

Just as I'm leaving I get a text from Taylor. It says she can't make it at 9:30. I'm kind of disappointed because I think she's hot, but I'm not going to complain because it certainly simplifies logistics for the evening.

I'm almost out the door when I get a second text from Taylor. It says: "C U 8:30."

Crap.

4

The rumor is true: Kayla knows how to kiss. We're sitting in the back row of a dark and mostly empty movie theater and we're certainly not watching the previews. She isn't one for small talk, it turns out, which is just fine by me because she's the best kisser so far. She's really full-on, the way I want to be, so it gives me a chance to move beyond Paige's sensitive approach and be full-on straight back at her.

"Hmmm," she says, pulling away. "Hold on there, tiger ... Try it like this instead." She leans back in.

I try it like that. It's even better than before. For almost three minutes I feel like I'm participating in a master class.

The opening credits for the movie have barely begun rolling when she pulls away again and whispers, "You'll never believe what I just found out."

"What's that?"

"I have the same measurements as—"

"Jessica Alba," I say, completing her sentence. "Or maybe Paris Hilton?"

She looks hurt. "No way. Same as Angelina Jolie ... when she's not pregnant, I mean."

"I got that."

"Yeah, so do you want to know what the measurements are?"

I attempt to sigh nonchalantly. "Sure, why not."

"36C-27-36."

I look down at her breasts. They do seem to be around 36C, but I know my credibility is at stake.

"Are you sure you're a 36C?"

"What kind of a question is that? That's like me asking you if you're sure your penis is six inches long."

I'm not actually sure my penis is six inches long, but I don't tell her that.

"I'm just saying I thought you might be more like a 36A or B."

"36A?" she spits. "What the f—"

Oops. "Probably 36B then."

"36B? Feel these and tell me they're 36B."

She turns to face me and I touch her breasts, but they're hidden beneath a hooded sweater, so I can't get a good read. This could work to my advantage.

"Too much padding," I explain, shaking my head.

"Too much padding for what?"

"For me to be able to judge."

Kayla looks away for a moment, then takes my hand and places it underneath her sweater. She lifts her bra and I'm touching her breast, and it's almost painfully erotic and—

"Are you satisfied now?" she asks in a vulnerable voice that catches me off guard.

I suppose the truthful answer is no, I want to spend the next ten minutes making up my mind, and then I want us to move on to third base. But in the dull light that flickers across her face, I can see that she's not enjoying this at all, and suddenly I feel mean and calculating and dirty. I don't want her to think of me that way, so I extricate my hand as surreptitiously as possible.

"Yeah," I whisper. "You were right…36C."

I'm hoping this will placate her, but it doesn't—she just nods curtly and turns to face the screen. I don't say anything else because her silence is cold and uninviting.

But then I look at my watch and realize it's almost eight o'clock, which gives me half an hour to develop a plan or I'll be leaving her in the middle of our date. And even though things haven't exactly gone well, that would be sure to annoy her.

And like I say, she's more muscular than me.

It's 8:10 and I haven't come up with a plan yet. I thought that Kayla might fall asleep from all our kissing, but three minutes of tonguing probably doesn't even count as a gentle warm-up for her. She's still watching the screen and we're still not talking.

I am, however, sweating.

8:20: I still haven't come up with a plan. I consider saying that I need to go to the bathroom, and then just not coming back. But if I do, then Kayla will have to inform the whole school that either (a) I'm wickedly constipated, or (b)

I found more than an hour's worth of alternative entertainment in a men's restroom. Neither of which is true.

I am, however, hyperventilating.

8:25: I've come to the realization that sometimes you just have to be a man and own up to your mistakes. And mine is that I've set up two dates with different girls on the same evening, which in the wider scheme of things—nuclear proliferation, third-world famine—isn't such a big deal. I'm sure Kayla will understand.

I am, however, scanning the theater for all nearby exits.

"So, K-Kayla," I croak. "You'll, um, never believe this, but—"

22

Kayla shushes me and I obediently shut up. I think she's actually into the movie. Onscreen, something exciting is about to happen; I can tell because the music is eerie, with trembling violins and sporadic trombone belches. Although it's entirely possible that I'm the only person in the theater thinking about the music.

8:27: Kayla gazes raptly at the movie couple. A tear falls from her eye, suggesting that she's currently emotionally vulnerable and therefore prone to kill the first person that pisses her off.

Which would be me.

"Kayla … Kayla … "

She shushes me again.

4

8:28: Kayla lowers her finger, giving me permission to speak.

"Kayla, I'm so sorry about this, but—"

Kayla's cellphone starts buzzing and she rips it from her pocket, flicking open the screen in one deft movement.

"Oh shit," she cries, just loud enough for everyone in the theater to hear.

"What is it?"

She looks at me, aghast. "My little sister's been kidnapped."

Okay, I have to admit I didn't see that one coming.

"I h-have to g-go," she gasps, standing awkwardly and grabbing her bag.

"Of course. God, I'm so sorry, Kayla, I really am. I hope she shows up soon."

I hope she shows up soon? Did I really just say that? What a retard.

"Yeah, sure," she grunts, looking at me like I'm a retard.

And then she's gone, and it's 8:29. I can't believe my luck. I make a mental note to thank Kayla's sister if she's found alive.

After a few seconds I exit the theater, emerging slowly in case Taylor is already waiting outside. The foyer is bustling, and it takes me a moment to see her standing beside a larger-than-life cardboard cutout of an anonymous superhero who's "KICKING BUTT ON JUNE 17!" The superhero is flanked by a couple of diminutive but largely naked women, which makes it even more impressive that Taylor commands

my complete attention. Her shiny red hair ripples
shoulders of a flowing, dark green dress, and a hea
chain and pendant gracefully adorn her neck. It's
that would really suit Abby.

"Hi, Taylor," I call out as I zip across the foyer.

"Oh, hi, Kevin." She pauses, a puzzled expression etched
on her face. "You'll never guess who I just saw running out
of here."

"Who?"

"Kayla. And she looked kind of freaked out."

"Really? That's too bad."

"Yeah. I hope she's okay."

Just in case she's thinking of continuing her inquiry further, I cough a couple of times to distract her.

"Are you okay? Do you have a cold?"

I shake my head. "No, it's nothing. So what do you want
to see?"

Taylor studies the list of movies and groans. "Geez, I
hate May."

"Huh?"

"May—I hate it. It's when they start wheeling out all the
made-for-morons blockbusters."

Nothing would make Taylor happier than to see the theater infested with a plague of costume dramas and Shake-
speare adaptations. After all, she has her thespian reputation
to uphold.

"Um, does anything appeal to you?"

She shakes her head and her hair shimmers like a Pan-
tene commercial. "Not really. Actually, I'd kind of prefer to

just hang out and talk. Maybe go get coffee. Would that be okay?"

Downer. Coffee shops aren't as conducive to groping as darkened movie theaters, so I'm not sure this plan is acceptable. But then I look at Taylor and say, "Yeah, sure," because she's just that hot. And at least this way I get seen with her in public.

Her favorite independent coffee shop is a couple blocks away in what used to be a church. Signs welcome us to the Buzz Shack, where stained-glass windows alternate with garish wall-hangings spouting slogans like "Jesus Supports Fair Trade Coffee" and "How Would Jesus Caffeinate?" Taylor notices me staring at them.

"Really get you thinking, don't they?" she says.

"Huh? Oh yeah. Definitely."

I look around and realize she's laughing at me, but not in an unfriendly way.

"I'm kidding, Kevin. I'm not even sure I'd read them until now."

I smile back. "So how *do* you think Jesus would caffeinate?"

She pauses to give the question due consideration. "I think he'd have to go at least a double latte—you know, to keep up the pep—and I guess he'd want iced, because it was pretty hot from what I hear."

When we reach the front of the line I order an iced double latte and Taylor has a giggling fit. When she can't gather herself after a few seconds, I go ahead and order the same thing for her. I tell the guy at the cash register, "It's what Jesus would want her to drink," and she loses it again.

While we wait for the barista to obsess over our drinks, I steal a glance at Taylor—she is, quite simply, stunning.

"I love your dress," I say, kind of hoping it sounds like a suave line.

"Thanks," she purrs. "I made it myself."

"What? No way!"

"Absolutely. I make a lot of my own clothes. Cheaper than a boutique, and you know they're going to fit."

"That's amazing."

I take a minute to study her dress. It's really impressive—not only does it fit her in ways I immediately appreciated, but it also lends a flow to her every movement. It even complements her hair color perfectly.

"I don't pretend to know anything about dresses, Taylor, but I'd have to say that you've got real talent."

She smiles and plays with her pendant. "Then we have something in common, don't we?"

"Oh yeah?" I really hope she's referring to my kissing technique.

"Yeah. Don't be modest. Everyone knows you're quite the accomplished flutist."

Ah, the flute—my partner in crime, and harbinger of doom when it comes to relationships. I hope she doesn't notice my shoulders slumping.

When we receive our lattes, Taylor invites me to pick a table, so I choose the one furthest away from the counter. It's quieter and seems a more likely venue for making out, even though there's a fresco of Jesus crucified just above our heads. When she sees it, Taylor opens her eyes super-wide and knits her thin eyebrows melodramatically, and I laugh again even though it feels a little weird with Jesus staring down at me.

"Does that come naturally," I ask, "or do you have to practice regularly?"

"What, the eyebrows? Oh yeah, an hour a day every day. My dad always told me: Taylor, master your eyebrows and the rest of acting will fall into place. And he's right. Acting's nothing but a series of well-timed eyebrow twitches."

She says everything so earnestly that it's almost possible to believe she means it. But then she breaks into a smile and her face lights up, and I want to kiss her really badly.

"So what about you, Kevin? Do you have to practice the flute as much as I practice my eyebrows?"

Ugh. There it is again—the flute. Not a good omen.

"Not really. Every now and then."

"Really? I mean, I heard your senior recital last semester. I thought it was incredible."

"You did?"

"Absolutely. I knew you were gifted, but I had no idea you were *that* good. Is it true you got an instrumental scholarship to Brookbank University?"

I shake my head. "Nah. Nothing like that," I say, surprised at how easily the lie slips out.

Taylor looks confused. "Oh, I guess I heard wrong…So do you still play in that pop group?"

"Huh?…Oh, the quartet. Yeah, but it's nothing much—"

"I thought you guys were really good last year. You know, when you played at the school fundraiser. You had real chemistry. Are you and Abby…close?"

Whoa. Tread carefully, Kevin. Spoiler alert!

"We're friends, that's all."

"Hmmm, that's fortunate."

For a moment we just look at each other, but then we start kissing for no other reason than we both know it's going to happen eventually, so we may as well get on with it. Taylor kisses delicately, so I revert to Paige mode for optimum results.

After a couple of minutes she pulls back, a sultry smile teasing the corners of her mouth. She points to a fresco on the opposite wall, depicting a nursing virgin Mary.

"I wonder if she was a 34C-25-35?"

I swallow hard. "Is that what you are?"

She turns back around to face me. "Uh-oh, I kind of let that one slip out, didn't I!"

"It's okay," I assure her. Because, well, it *is* okay.

"Yeah, but…" She looks away.

We sit in silence for a while. Occasionally I lean forward optimistically, but she doesn't seem to pick up on my body language; maybe her internal translator is malfunctioning or something. Eventually the silence becomes oppressive, so I say the first thing that comes into my head:

"What happened to you and Zach?"

She looks surprised, but recovers quickly. "A few weeks ago he started acting weird, saying he couldn't really commit anymore. He was a real jerk about it, so I broke up with him."

"Um, yeah. So why'd you go out with him, anyhow?"

"Do we have to talk about Zach?"

No, we don't. Now that I've discovered her measurements, my only interest is in confirming those measurements through the medium of my own two hands. But because this concerns Zach, my self-esteem won't let me leave it alone.

"You must have seen something in him to date him for almost a year."

"Zach can be generous."

"That's it?"

She narrows her eyes. "You really want to know? Fine. I dated him because his dad is an orthodontist, and I got free dental work while we were dating. Satisfied now?"

"You're not serious."

"I'm totally serious." She sighs. "I needed orthodontic work and my family couldn't afford it. Why do you think I make my own clothes?"

I shake my head vacantly.

"Look, I'm the oldest of six kids and my dad's a carpenter, so cosmetic dentistry comes way down the list for us. But I was told that if I'm ever going to have a future as an actress, I kind of needed to have the work done, even though I hate it that crap like that might actually matter."

I check out her teeth. They're definitely white and straight, although I still think the price may have been a little steep.

"Well, you have beautiful teeth now," I assure her. "But I thought you were beautiful before you had any work done."

Taylor smiles coyly. "Kevin Mopsely, I do declare you've made me blush," she drawls in what I think is an impersonation of Scarlett from *Gone with the Wind*.

"Sorry," I say, even though I'm not.

"Quite all right ... You probably think I'm a complete slut for using Zach, don't you?"

"No way. I think you're a saint for putting up with him all year."

"That's nice, but I don't think Zach would see it that way if he knew." Her eyes grow wide again. "You won't tell him, will you? Promise."

"I promise I won't tell him, although I think he'd say it was worth it anyway. I mean, he got to date Taylor Carson for most of senior year."

Taylor looks surprised. "Thanks for saying that."

"It's true."

We avoid eye contact as we slurp the last few drops of our lattes.

"You know, you're a really good listener," she says.

"A better listener than kisser?" I ask provocatively.

"Yeah, a better listener." *Naaaah. Incorrect response. Try again.* "And that's a really good thing. Anyone can learn to be a good kisser, but not everyone's a good listener."

I understand her logic, but it's not quite in line with my aspirations.

"I'm serious, Kevin," she adds, watching my face. "Give me a listener over a kisser any day."

"Okay."

Taylor glances at her watch. "Look, I've still got some homework to do, so I'd better be going."

"Yeah, sure."

She leans across the table and plants a kiss on my cheek. It says we're friends, nothing more. Which is exactly what I've come to expect from dates. Until now it hasn't even bothered me that much. But as she stands up, I feel a pang of regret.

And then she sits back down, stares off into the distance, and shakes her head.

"Why are you with them, Kevin? Brandon and Zach and all the others. They're jerks, you know. And you're not."

"They're not really jerks."

She gives a hollow laugh. "Wow. The lies we tell to get what we want."

"What, like me being a good listener?"

"No, Kevin," she snaps. "Like you pretending they're good guys."

"They are."

"Sure they are. And I'm a 34C-25-35."

"Oh, so you're not?"

"No, I'm not."

Suddenly Taylor sounds quite angry, and I'm not entirely sure why. She tugs at the shoulders of her dress, like she feels exposed and wants to cover up.

"Those are the measurements that the fashion magazines want me to have, but the only way I'll ever get there is if I eat one stick of celery a day and get breast implants." She looks exasperated. "If you really want to know, I'm a 34B-28-38. And if that's all you see when you look at me then go ahead and use the numbers, 'cause I'm not willing to play this game anymore."

I don't like the way this conversation is going.

"But … you're beautiful," I say smoothly, hoping she doesn't really know what I suspect she knows. "Anyway, I don't care about your measurements."

She shakes her head angrily. "Then why are you putting

us all through this, huh? Why are you making us so defensive about our bodies?"

It's like I'm listening to my mom. Why couldn't we have ended this a few minutes ago?

"What are you talking about, Taylor?"

"Oh, drop the innocent act. We all know you're the one compiling the Book of Busts. Why do you think you've had so many dates the past two weeks?"

Oh crap. This is bad. And she's not done yet.

"And just so you know," she fumes, "after every date you've been on we compare notes so we can get our numbers to you with as little kissing and groping as possible. And we try to make suggestions to you so the next girl who goes out with you doesn't have to put up with you sticking your tongue straight down her throat, like you did with Paige. Or mashing her breasts, like you did with Jessica."

Oh geez. This is horrible. And she's still not done.

"You don't feel any guilt at all, do you? None of you do. A month ago I was comfortable with my body. But then Zach started acting weird, and you began compiling this book, and suddenly I'm worried that my tits are too small and my waist is too large. I can't even eat lunch in the cafeteria anymore because I'm paranoid that people are watching me, thinking I eat too much. Do you have any idea what that's like?"

"I'm sorry," I say simply.

"No, you're not. But you should be. Because you haven't just made us hate ourselves, you've made us hate you as well...For some reason, I didn't think you'd sell out so cheaply."

"What does that mean?"

"It means we all know who you are, Kevin. You're supposed to be one of the smartest boys in our class, and you're the best musician any of us has ever known. I wasn't the only girl at your recital, and all of us thought you were amazing. If you'd ever bothered to speak to us we'd have told you so to your face. But you never did. And the worst thing is, you actually think we'll like you more now that you're acting like a complete jerk." She gesticulates wildly with her hands, reverting to cheerleader mode. "Oh yeah, that's cute, that's endearing. Please, sign me up for a boyfriend like that!"

"You had a boyfriend like that, in case you haven't noticed."

"Yes, I did. But not because I wanted to. And I know that makes me slutty, and I hate that, but Zach deserved nothing better. At least that's what I thought. But now I'm starting to think he actually did deserve to be treated better than you."

I can't hide my surprise. "And how do you figure that?"

"Because he's too stupid to know any better. He's too ignorant to be kind and gentle and thoughtful. And so are all those other Neanderthals you're hanging out with. But you know better than them. You're not ignorant. And in my opinion, that makes you a thousand times worse than they are."

Taylor storms off before I can utter a word in my defense. Which is probably just as well, because I'm not sure I have one.

23

"Truce?" says Abby, twisting her mouth into a smile.

We've just finished a really polished rendition of "California Dreamin'" and she's using the positive vibe to break the ice. I look around, but Nathan and Caitlin have already snuck away to make out.

"Look, Kev, I'm sorry I gave you a hard time last week. I guess it's none of my business who you hang out with. I only said it because I think you're better than those guys."

I watch her closely to gauge whether she and Taylor are in league together, but I don't think so. Besides, Abby would probably never talk to me again if she knew I'd kissed four girls in seven days. I can hardly blame her.

"Yo, Kev. Did you hear what I said?"

"Oh yeah…" I try to remember what she just said— something about me being a good guy. "I mean, yeah, thanks."

"So are we good?"

"Yeah, we're good," I assure her.

"So we're on for Saturday?"

"Saturday?"

"You know … third Saturday of the month." She waits expectantly for me to fill in the rest. I fail. "It's curry night, you dope. Crazy British tradition featuring blindingly spicy food and strongly alcoholic beer."

"Oh, of course. Yeah, we're definitely on."

"Great. Is your mom still sticking to her don't-ask-don't-tell policy on the booze?"

"I think so."

"Well, cheers to that." She raises her hand in mock toast.

In the silence that follows, I watch Abby wrap a stray curl behind her ear. It's a motion as familiar to me as the sound of her voice, and for a moment I can almost convince myself that nothing at all has changed between us.

"Hey, Abby … "

"Yeah?"

"I'm sorry for what I said the other night … You were right, I didn't have the balls to tell the guys no, even though I know I should've."

I must look depressed, because Abby stands behind me and massages my shoulders.

"It's never too late," she whispers.

"So Spud, any progress?" beams Brandon.

"Dude," nods Spud.

148

"Can we see something... anything?"

"*Dude*," warns Spud.

Brandon sighs, accepting that this is Spud's final—and only, it would seem—word on the matter. He turns to face me and I take a deep breath.

In my dreams I'd visualized this moment, the one when I fill the guys in on Taylor's measurements. I'd look straight at Zach, invoke the name "Taylor Carson" with delicious emphasis, give them her numbers, and then provide a detailed account of the circumstances under which I came to uncover those numbers. And all the while Zach would be squirming, knowing that I'd one-upped him.

But that was before the date actually happened. The reality is that I've been repeatedly reliving Taylor's blistering attack, and it's as much as I can do to say the numbers for her and Kayla without flaking out.

The halfhearted smattering of applause quickly fades. I notice there are fewer of us now. Most of the football team has drifted away and I'm not sure why.

Brandon looks confused. He turns to Zach and cocks an eyebrow inquiringly.

"What? So I dumped her," grunts Zach.

"Oh yeah? Well, now she's auditioning for the role of Mrs. Mopsely." Brandon claps me on the back. "So you went to second with Taylor, huh? Zach dates her for a year and gets nowhere, but one date with you and she's ready to give it up."

I ought to tell him that he couldn't be more wrong, but I just can't.

Meanwhile, Zach stares at me with festering hatred.

"And what about Abby?" he quips. "I don't see her numbers. You must have had her a ton of times by now."

"No," I say, loathing Zach for dragging her name into the discussion.

"Oh, come on. I mean, she must be so desperate for it she'd bed anyone. Do you want one of us to take care of her for you? Because if you're not up to it we're here for you, just like Brandon said. You know that, right?"

"I don't need any of you to take care of her, as you put it. When I find out her … her dimensions, I'll tell you—"

"Her *dimensions*? You make her sound like a boat. Which I guess is pretty close—"

"Just leave her out of this!"

"Ooooh, look who's getting all moody." Zach waves his hands back and forth like he's Homer Simpson. "Is it that time of the month, Kevin?"

"Screw you."

Zach smiles. "Know what I think? I think the reason you haven't got Abby's scores yet is 'cause she's a dyke. That's what I heard, anyway."

"And I heard you're an ignorant jerk. Go figure."

"That's not a denial though—"

"Yeah, it's a denial. 'Cause I'm seeing her on Saturday, if you must know."

Zach shuts up, but he continues to smirk shamelessly. And then I notice that Brandon's laughing too, which annoys me a whole lot more.

24

"Eyup," grunts Abby's dad as he wrestles the front door open.

Richard, as he insists on my calling him, is short and red-cheeked like an animated garden gnome. He's also pretty toasted.

He winks conspiratorially. "Don't tell the missus, but I'm pretty toasted."

"Really?" I gasp, like this hasn't happened the three previous times I've attended curry night.

"'Fraid so, mate. Slaughtered, I am. Wankered, wasted, and generally whammed. Good stuff, though," he adds, waving an empty pint glass in front of my face. "Fancy one?"

"Sure." I try to say it as nonchalantly as possible, but it still feels weird to be in a house where the British drinking age is in effect.

"Pick your poison, son." He waves an arm in the direction

of the sideboard; it's swamped by dozens of beer bottles, all with lewd or lascivious names.

I look for one I recognize but I must seem completely lost, because he wraps an arm around me paternally and points at the first bottle. "Tasty little laugh and titter, this one."

"He means it's a good bitter," translates Abby, sliding over to join us. "Your typical amber-colored beer, full-bodied, low alcohol content."

I look admiringly at her and, well...she looks really good. I'm not even sure why. Maybe it's the hair, still slightly damp and rippling over her shoulders.

"Did you do something to your hair?" I ask.

"Yeah, I washed it," she says, stifling a laugh.

"Oh."

Silence.

"And this little number is a corking salmon and trout from Scouse country," says Richard, continuing from right where he left off.

"Which means it's a fine stout from Liverpool, in the north of England," Abby explains. "It's dark, rich, smooth, and you'll be wasted before you finish the first pint."

"I'll have one of those, thanks," I say, rather liking the sound of that.

"And I'll have an Old Thumper," chirps Abby.

I figure I've misheard her. "A what?"

"An Old Thumper. It's another strong ale." She winks. "I wouldn't want you to feel like you're going it alone this evening."

Richard decants the beer into pint glasses with as much

care as he can, but he's so far gone it doesn't go too well. Several generous droplets tumble onto the hardwood floor and are quickly claimed by Beckham, Abby's alcoholic beagle.

"Don't worry," Abby reassures me. "You know that Beckham's used to it. His tolerance is legendary." She lowers her voice. "Although I'd appreciate it if you could keep an eye on Dad at the end of the evening."

"Why's that?"

She frowns. "He has a habit of pouring the leftover beer into Beckham's bowl. Sometimes we don't see the poor thing again until Wednesday."

Beckham looks up at me plaintively. I think he's actually using doggie telepathy to tell me to drop some more beer, and I burst out laughing.

"Don't give him any," Abby teases me. "I know what you're thinking." She intertwines her arm with mine and we walk into the dining room, where about twenty Styrofoam containers jostle for space on the table.

"Ready for a shit in a hurry?" Richard chortles.

"Richard!" gasps Abby's mom, Samantha, also red-cheeked.

"What? A shit in a hurry means curry. It's perfectly kosher Cockney rhyming slang, Sam."

"I don't care," warns Sam. "We have a guest, remember? Hello, Kevin, how are you?" She gives me a bear hug and kisses both cheeks as Abby sniggers in the background.

"Good, thanks, Samantha."

"Call me Sam. You'll find it easier to manage as you make your way through that there beer."

"You'd better Adam and Eve it," agrees Richard.

"He means you'd better believe it," says Abby.

"'Cause that's wicked strong stuff, Kev. One moment you're nattering away without a care in the world, the next moment everything's gone totally pear-shaped."

I wait for Abby to translate, but she just crosses her eyes and shrugs. We both laugh. It's only when we stop that I notice our legs are touching under the table.

We stay that way for the rest of the meal.

❋

"You two can leave the table if you want," says Sam. "You know what Richard's like . . . won't stop until everything's been eaten. And then he'll spend the rest of the weekend moaning about his curry bottom."

"Too much information, Mom," groans Abby.

"Ha! If you think that's too much information, imagine what it's like having to deal with it!"

"Aaaaargh! Way too much information, Mom."

Abby grabs my hand and pulls me away playfully. We run upstairs to her bedroom, and she leads me over to the window.

"That's where you stand when we talk," she says, pointing next door.

I squint at my own room and realize that I can see straight into my closet. I really need some new clothes.

"You really need some new clothes," she says.

"Hmmm."

We're still holding hands, and I don't want to let go.

"Did you get enough to eat?" she asks.

"Yeah."

"What about your drink? Do you want me to go get it for you? Or I could get you a new one, 'cause there's plenty left…"

Abby's babbling, and since Abby never babbles it can only mean she's nervous. And I think I might know what she's nervous about. She blinks a few times as I gaze at her, then swallows hard.

"No, I'm fine, thanks," I tell her, because if I'm right, I want to be sober.

Neither of us moves for a moment, so I lean forward and kiss her cheek hopefully, expectantly. I can hear her swallowing, or maybe that's me. My pulse races. Abby doesn't respond at first, but then she turns her head slightly, her cheek nudging against mine. I smell the almond scent of her hair, feel the softness of her skin. And her head continues to turn. And so does mine.

I close my eyes the moment her lips brush against mine. It feels like we've still got miles to go, and for once I don't want to hurry the journey. Even when our lips come fully together I don't open my mouth until Abby does, and the lightning-strike of tongue-against-tongue leaves me breathless.

Slowly, gently, our bodies join as well. I can feel her chest against me, the warmth of her body next to mine. For a good long while this is everything we want, everything we need, and we dwell in the perfection of the moment.

Even when the connection breaks, we part easily. Abby takes a deep breath and smiles—a wide smile, an honest smile, and I notice that her skin creases from the corners of her mouth up to her nose. The creases are deep because she spends so much of her life smiling, which seems like a really good thing.

"Wow. Where did you learn to kiss like that?" I say.

She places a finger on my lips. "It's best not to ask a girl a question like that."

We come back together with mouths open and ready. Her tongue brushes back and forth against mine, dancing with an intensity that seems new and electric. She wraps a hand behind my head, pulling me closer, even though we can't get any closer. Only I know exactly what it is she wants to feel, so I forget about Paige's sensitive approach and Kayla's palette of full-on techniques and just do whatever feels right.

For a moment I'm aware that it's the first time I've been kissing without thinking about the fact that I'm kissing, which makes it even better. And we don't part after a minute, or two, or three. I can't even say how long we remain where we are, kissing by her bedroom window like it's the only thing in the world that really matters.

Without awkwardness, Abby pulls back and smiles. She links her fingers with mine and leads me over to the door, which she closes and locks.

I swallow hard. "Won't your parents—"

"They like you, Kevin. They trust you. And they, um . . . aren't like most parents."

I think I know what she's saying, so I just nod and follow as she leads me over to her bed. She lays down and pulls me on top of her and immediately we're kissing again. I run my hand through her soft hair, following the contours of her ear, the nape of her neck, the curve of her shoulder. As if on remote control, my hand carries on down until it reaches her bra strap; a moment later, it cups her breast. A barely audible sound seems to emerge from somewhere deep inside her, and while I'm no expert, I'm fairly certain it's a really good sound.

Abby opens her eyes, and for a few seconds she simply watches me, smiling like she needs me to know this is okay, this is *shared*. She reaches up and touches my face, exploring me through the delicate motions of her fingertips, then reaches down and unbuttons my shirt. She runs her fingers over my chest and slides my shirt off surprisingly smoothly. When I hesitate to reciprocate, she guides my hands to the buttons on her own shirt, breathing heavily as I fumble to remove it. Her skin is so soft, so smooth, so pale. I've never felt so utterly turned on.

She rolls us over so I'm underneath, then kisses my chest. I brush my fingers across her breasts again, and she reaches back and unclips her bra. It falls onto my chest.

"You can touch them," she whispers.

I nod dumbly, tracing the contours of each breast with a single finger. I can feel her watching me, and for a split second I can't help grinning. I'm afraid it'll ruin the atmosphere, but Abby just grins back, laughing her gentle, throaty laugh. And that's when it hits me … making out with Abby feels as naturally comfortable as talking to her. There's no awkwardness between us, just a craving to know each other completely. It's the most beautiful thing I've ever experienced.

Sensing my distraction, Abby runs the back of her hand

across my face, then presses herself against me, kissing me forcefully. I kiss her right back and we tangle our bodies together. When I finally open my eyes, Abby's face beams down at me.

"Hey, you," she says.

"Hey, you." I'm beaming too.

She lies down beside me, rests her head in her hand. She's too beautiful for words.

"Thank you," I say finally, even though it feels wrong to break the perfect silence.

"For what?"

"For this."

She nods, and the corners of her mouth turn up slightly. "So what exactly *is* this?"

I watch her to see if she's teasing, but that would be too easy. This time she actually wants me to say it, to spell it out and make it real.

"This is … us," I say. "And I like us. I like us more than I like just you and me."

Abby smiles. "Good, 'cause I like us too."

I don't want to move. I don't want to speak. I just want us to stay where we are, forever. But then Abby looks away.

"Just give me a moment, okay?" she whispers, biting her lip.

As I nod, she gets up and walks into her bathroom. It seems an odd time to need to pee, but I'm in such a blissful mood that even impromptu trips to the toilet can't spoil the moment.

I hear her flick the light switch, and a cupboard door creaks open. Then I notice her bra beside me on the bed and pick it up. It's really fancy, with surprisingly soft lacy borders. There's no padding at all, which makes me wonder what size it is—a 36B, I'd guess. I turn it over and squint at the label on the strap, trying to make out the numbers in the semidarkness.

"What are you doing?"

I freeze, then drop the bra and look over my shoulder. Abby stands beside me, still topless, her skin glowing in the low light.

"Nothing. I wasn't doing anything."

She's crying. I've never seen her cry before, but now I can see the tears running down her cheeks as though attempting a desperate flight from her eyes. I can't breathe.

"You were looking at my bra."

"Yeah, but—"

"You were looking to see what size I am." She bites her lip as her face crumples. "It's true, isn't it?"

I don't want to lie to her, so I just nod.

"How could you do this to me? How could you do it to *me*?"

"What do you mean?"

"You know what I mean, Kevin," she hisses, her features wrought with pain. "Please, whatever you do, don't patronize me."

"I'm not patronizing you," I insist, suddenly grateful that she doesn't know about the Book of Busts. "I just don't understand why—"

"I know about the Book of Busts."

Crap. At least she doesn't know about the dates.

"And I know about your dates with Paige and Jessica and Kayla and Taylor."

Big crap. At least she doesn't know about them comparing notes.

"And I've heard them comparing notes on you, laughing at you, saying you were so useless they even had to teach you how to kiss and how to touch them. And I've kept telling myself they're wrong, that you're kind and sensitive and talented and interesting, that this... this *new* version of you is nothing but an act. I knew if only I could get you alone you'd be yourself again, because you'd never betray me. But now I..." she chokes and the words won't come out "... now I realize I'm no different than the others—"

"No, no. You're wrong. You *are* different." I shuffle along the bed, trying to put some distance between myself and the offending bra. "I'd never add your... size to the book. I'd never do it. Not to you."

"That's not the point, Kevin. The point is that during the most wonderful evening of my life, you had to go and check my bra size like it actually means something. For a few minutes there you made me feel special... sexy. Now I just feel slutty... God, I can't believe you've made me feel this way."

I'm breathing fast and my mouth is dry, but I manage to find the words I'm looking for. "Please, Abby. You have to believe me—I never meant to look. I don't know why I did. I mean, I think... I think this last week I've begun to realize that I might... I kind of might... love you."

Abby picks up my shirt and hands it to me. "That's beautiful, Kevin. That's so touching. You *think* that you kind of *might* love me. Wow." She turns away and shakes her head, then faces me again with a look of utter disdain. "Just for the record," she chokes, "I *know* that I love you, and I've loved you for almost a year. So pardon me if I say that that isn't as complimentary as you'd like it to be."

"Please, Abby—"

"Just go, Kevin. I need to be alone. And you need to go work out who the hell you really are."

I pull on my shirt, and I'm about to exit when Abby tosses me something. It's a square foil packet, and although I've never used one before, I know it's a condom. She wasn't peeing in the bathroom—she was getting contraception in case she went all the way.

With me.

"You may as well take that with you," she whispers. "Maybe you can use it on your next date."

I run out and take the stairs two at a time. I know I ought to stop and thank her parents, but by the time I reach the door to the dining room I'm too ashamed to see them, so I just hurry by and let myself out.

I make it up to my bedroom without being intercepted by Mom. The packet still clenched in my hand reminds me of Abby, so I look out at her bedroom window, but the blind is closed. Behind it, the only girl who has ever liked me for myself is crying herself to sleep.

25

Taylor's no longer attending English. Neither is Jessica. Paige realizes that she and Morgan are the final holdouts and starts fiddling with her cigarettes.

Ms. Kowalski has clearly anticipated this reduced class. She enters with a triumphant flourish, throwing her bag onto the desk with a satisfying thump. I notice she's wearing her white blouse again, and that the stain from the black dry-erase marker didn't completely come out. Paige notices too. She points a finger, chuckling forcefully.

"What's so amusing, Paige?" asks Ms. K.

"Nothing...Well, actually, it's your blouse. It has black stains across the back."

A few of the guys laugh, not because it's funny but because they've been conditioned to respond to Paige's attacks with Pavlovian consistency. Ms. K says nothing, just nods and turns her back to us so that we can see what Paige is talking about.

"Do you all see it?" she says, turning around to face us. "The stain, I mean. My blouse got stained the first time I wore it, but I still wear it anyway. I suppose that makes me a bad person. Perhaps it means I'm unfashionable, unpopular, and have no life. Perhaps if I simply disposed of the blouse and bought a new one I could prove my intense self-awareness, my slavish attention to appearances, my infatuation with superficiality." She furrows her eyebrows as though deep in thought. "Yes, that would certainly make me a vastly superior human being."

I figure that no one understands a word she's saying, or even that she's being sarcastic. But as I look around I realize that for once I'm wrong—at least half of the guys have their eyes cast down, embarrassed for having laughed.

Paige appears completely unapologetic. In her world, she's guilty of nothing more than stating the truth. She may even believe—in her twisted, pathologically bitchy way— that she has saved Ms. K from perpetuating an obviously unforgivable fashion error.

But Ms. K isn't looking at Paige—she's staring straight at me.

Slowly and deliberately I lower my eyes, too, because on some deep level I need her to know that I know Paige is wrong, and she is right.

"How was school?" Mom asks, handing me a slice of pizza.

"Fine."

"What do you mean by 'fine'?"

"I mean the tolerable and the intolerable parts of my day canceled each other out," I say, sure that this is not the definition she's been looking for every night.

Matt the Mutt growls at me because I've raised my voice. He's been seeking retribution ever since the lasagna incident. I fully expect Mom to start growling at me too, but she just laughs.

"What?" I say, unamused.

"Oh, Kevin, I'm sorry. You seem so miserable at the moment, and I can't help laughing because I'm clearly having a much better time at your school than you are. I mean, you have to enjoy the unlikelihood of it."

I don't have to enjoy it at all. "What's so great about Brookbank High?"

"It's my class. You may have noticed that my numbers just keep growing, and there's clearly a very genuine and justified discontent seething among the girls at your school."

"Hmmm."

"And they're just so thoughtful and forthright. I wish my undergrads were half as engaged as these girls are. Just today they decided they needed a name ... you know, as a symbol of their solidarity. Someone came up with Brookbankers Against Boys Espousing Stereotypes, but then we had a discussion on why the acronym BABES might not be conducive to our agenda of viewing ourselves as more than sexual objects. So someone else suggested Girls Rejecting Really Lewd Stereotypes."

"GRRLS?"

"Yes, you know … 'GRRLS' is the hip, culturally relevant acronym signifying postpubescent female self-affirmation."

"What?"

"Never mind. Point is, they really thought about it, like it *mattered* to them. It's the first time in years I've felt like I'm actually making a difference."

"That's great," I say, even though none of this is reassuring me in the slightest.

"Yes, and then after today's class the captain of the cheerleading squad came along and asked if she could join us."

I try not to choke on a slice of pepperoni. "Morgan Giddes?"

"Yes. We had a nice chat. She's such an erudite young woman." Mom sighs. "I must admit, I had her all wrong when she walked through the door. I just figured someone that popular and attractive was not exactly my target audience. But the longer we talked, the more I realized she's probably as attuned to the way girls at your school are mistreated and misrepresented as anyone in the class. It's inspiring."

I'm trying to reconcile this appraisal with my own knowledge of Morgan, which pretty much amounts to ogling her from across crowded rooms. And then I remember Brandon.

"But she's dating … well, her boyfriend is, um—"

"A butthole, right? Yes, she mentioned him. And it's not the first time his name has come up in my class, believe me." She shakes like the room just got cold. "It sounds like he's a truly narcissistic, offensive, sexist pig."

She looks to me for confirmation, so I smile ambivalently.

"But don't worry," Mom continues cheerily. "She's not with Brandon anymore. She said he got angry with her when she wouldn't let him touch her breasts, and he called her 'tight' and other awful things, so she told him to get lost. I have to admit, I cheered when she told me that."

Uh-oh.

26

I keep waiting for everyone else to show up for the Rituals meeting, as the present group consists of the offensive line from the football team, the starters on the baseball team, and me. As if I didn't already feel like a total outsider, this seals the deal. Meanwhile, Brandon paces around the room.

"Hey, Brandon," shouts one of his teammates. "Have you got Morgan's stats yet?"

"Huh? Oh yeah, Morgan." Brandon laughs. "Yeah, I got her stats all right. But I got to check them again, if you know what I'm saying. And then again, and again." He thrusts his pelvis forward suggestively as Zach fawns by his side.

"We don't need you to check your numbers a hundred times. Just give Kevin the scores. Come on, it's not fair for you to keep them to yourself."

Brandon looks at me like I'm the one who just said it, and the atmosphere suddenly seems tense.

"Hey, just leave Brandon alone," I say, surprised by the sound of my own voice. "When he's ready, he'll tell us, okay?"

"Yeah, Kev's right," says Brandon, eager to change the subject. He coughs and turns to me. "So, you got Abby's scores yet?"

I can't believe he's asking me this after I just saved his butt. "No, I don't have Abby's scores."

"But you said you and her were hanging out on Saturday. Don't tell me you struck out."

Zach's smirking in Brandon's shadow. I want to tell them both to get lost.

"No, I didn't strike out."

A horrified look envelops Brandon's face. "You got caught stealing second!"

I try to stay cool, try to ignore the hypocrisy. "No, I just didn't want to go to second base."

"All right, that's cool. I don't blame you really, 'cause let's be honest ... she's not exactly the hottest girl in school. She's not going to win any beauty contests, that's for sure."

"If you think she's ugly, you should see her parents," Zach interjects. "They're freaks. Like, seriously, their teeth are freakin' bent all over the place and yellow and shit. My dad's an orthodontist and when he saw them he just laughed and said it's proof that Britain's like a third-world country."

Zach laughs, and Brandon laughs, and gradually everyone else joins in too because they're afraid they may have missed a classic comedy moment. But this time I don't join them, even though Zach is staring at me.

"Sorry, Kev," he smirks. "Did I offend you talking about your girlfriend's parents like that?"

"She's not my girlfriend, and no, you didn't offend me. I just never thought anyone would be dumb enough to say that straight white teeth are the defining characteristic of developed nations." I try to sound like my mom so that Zach will appear stupid. It works—he goes bright red.

"So you're saying their teeth look okay, is that it?"

"No, I'm not. Sure, their teeth are freaky enough to scare small children, but that's not the point. The point is that you're too stupid and vain and fixated on teeth to know that you're talking complete crap. You're so dumb you didn't even realize Taylor was—"

Uh-oh. I stop mid-sentence, hold my breath and wonder how to continue. I can't mention what Taylor said—I promised I wouldn't. And even though she humiliated me the other night, I actually feel sympathy for her, having to date Zach for a year just to get free dental work.

"I didn't realize Taylor was *what?*" snarls Zach.

"That she was ... was ... a feminist."

There's a collective gasp like I just called her a leper, and then Ryan's laughing and pointing at Zach.

"You dated a feminist for an entire year and you didn't even realize it, you pussy!"

Everyone else joins in the laughter like the obedient little sheep they are, and I breathe a sigh of relief.

As we file out of the room, I see Abby standing in the corridor. I think she's waiting for me, and although I'm scared to death about what she's going to say, I want to apologize to her. I *need* to apologize.

I'm about to join her when Brandon wraps an arm around my shoulders.

"You should be a comedian, Kev. For real. Like, that thing you said about Abby's parents—their teeth are freaky enough to scare small children—absolutely hilarious!"

I feel my body go rigid.

Brandon lets go, surprised. "What's the matter?" He looks up, sees Abby, and laughs nervously. "Whoa! Fucked up!" He laughs again, but Abby's mouth just hangs open in shock. "What? Come on, like it's not true."

Abby spins on her heel and hurries down the corridor. I want to run after her, but if I do it will confirm everything Zach just said about her being my girlfriend—and for the rest of the year she'll be abused by Zach and Brandon and probably everyone else, even though she's done nothing wrong. So I stay rooted to the spot.

"Ugly *and* weird," Brandon concludes as her figure recedes into the distance.

"No, she's not," I say. Only Brandon's not listening, because Brandon never listens.

"Don't forget the baseball semis tomorrow," he shouts as he walks away. "Games like this are where legends are born."

I nod, but in the back of my mind all I can think about is how Mom was right: Brandon can be a real asshole.

27

I've decided to leave the quartet. Nobody actually knows this yet, but they'll find out after school today when I don't show up for practice.

It's not that I'm a coward—it's just that I'm too frightened to face Abby. Come to think of it, I'm too scared to face a lot of people right now: Paige, Jessica, Kayla, Taylor, Zach. I'm even avoiding Spud. I don't know if he and Zach are close, but if they are it stands to reason that Zach would get Spud to carry out his ritual slayings for him, sort of like the Mafia.

During English, I start counting down the school days that are left: only seven until prom, and then fifteen after that. I could fake a mystery virus for three days without arousing suspicion, but that still leaves nineteen school days, and that's nineteen too many. I'm wondering if it's possible to graduate if I miss the last month of school. Sure, my class ranking would tank, but that's a totally acceptable trade.

It was just last week that I didn't want school to end. I had dreams of five more pre-prom dates—109 in a parallel universe. I imagined my life chronicled in the annals of Brookbank High—a Lothario, a stud. Turns out it was just early onset insanity. But I've returned to reality. Now I just want to disappear. Maybe by the time I resurface, nobody will remember I ever existed.

I don't speak during English, and neither does Paige. I think it's starting to dawn on her that being the only girl in class is actually quite daunting, especially as most of the guys spend the whole time shamelessly checking her out. She sits in her customary seat at the back of the room, but it doesn't matter—they just rubberneck anyway. Without any of her friends around, she can't even complain aloud as they ogle her. I wonder how much longer she'll hold out.

I'm almost out the school door when I see Nathan studying the vending machine options. I feel a pang of guilt, knowing I'm about to stand him and the other quartet members up, so I hurry over, hoping I can make amends preemptively.

"Hey, Nathan. What are you getting?" I ask nonchalantly.

"Oh, hey. Geez, I don't know. Something Diet ... Diet Sprite."

Before he can say another word, I press the Diet 7-Up

and Diet Coke buttons, then bang the Diet Sprite button with my knee. There's an ominous cracking sound like I may have applied a little too much pressure, but the can obediently rolls out anyway.

Nathan doesn't move. "Wow. You hit the machine... and there's a can."

"Yes," I say, handing it to him.

"What did you just do?"

"Um, I can't tell you. I promised I wouldn't show anyone."

"I'm not talking about your trick—the knee-strike, the button bang—I'm talking about stealing."

I can feel his disapproval like a chill in the air. "No, Nathan. It's not like that. The guy who owns the vending machine is cool with it."

"Oh, really?"

"Yeah. He uses the missing cans as an excuse to fire people he doesn't like." Nathan studies me like I'm growing an extra head. "Oh, man, that didn't come out right. Look, I just figured you'd like a freebie, that's all."

Nathan narrows his eyes and carefully flattens his hair with his fingertips. "Let me recap, Kev. You're stealing drinks, but it's cool 'cause you're also helping Mr. Vending Machine fire his employees. Any of this sounding illegal... unethical?"

"No way. It's not like that..."

He gives me a couple seconds to continue, then hands the can back.

"Keep it. This one's a little too cold for me."

4

"How was school?" Mom asks.

"Fine."

"What do you mean by 'fine'?"

Not again. I'm about to scream when I notice she's laughing.

"I'm just kidding, honey." She taps away on the computer keyboard. "I thought you'd be disappointed if I didn't ask you about your day."

"No, not disappointed at all," I assure her.

"Oh. Well, it would be nice to hear you say something about school every now and then."

"Okay. How about, I'm ready for graduation."

"Ha ha. You seniors are all the same. My new student, Morgan, said she's ready to move on too. She said she's even sick of cheerleading—she wants to get back to solo dance so she can express herself outside of the prescribed boundaries of micromanaged routines."

"She really said that?"

"Uh-huh. She also said the boys at Brookbank make her feel uncomfortable, like she's nothing more than an object for their twisted fantasies, although I think she was generalizing. I mean, you'd never make a girl feel like a fantasy object, and there must be other boys like you."

"Hmmm."

"Oh, that reminds me," Mom says excitedly, returning her attention to the computer. "Jane said they'd put some information about my class on the school Web site."

Suddenly my heart is racing. "It doesn't say anything about me, does it?"

"I don't know, but I expect so. Let's find out."

Mom closes her e-mail and pulls up Google. She begins to enter the name of the school, but after she types the first two letters, the computer completes the search term for her: *breast measurements examples with images*. She stops typing and reads the words over and over, as if trying to divine some deep and hidden meaning.

"Why does it say 'breast measurements examples with images,' Kevin?"

"Um, I don't know. You typed it in, not me."

"No, I typed in 'br,' the computer filled in the rest."

"That's weird."

"Kevin, you don't use the computer to … you know … self-stimulate, do you?"

"Oh my God."

"I mean, I want you to know that it's perfectly healthy for a boy your age to masturbate, but since we both share the computer, it would make me feel a little uncomfortable to imagine you sitting here—"

"Can we please not talk about this?"

Mom huffs. "No, honey, I think we need to get this out in the open. You've been behaving strangely lately, and now I find you've been using the Internet to locate soft porn. You know I don't approve of the male fascination with breasts, any more than the vagina or clitoris—"

"We're not having this conversation."

"Oh yes we are, Kevin. You've changed, and I want to know why."

"I haven't changed."

"Kevin!" snaps Mom, but then there's knocking on the front door so she gets up to answer it. "Don't think we won't revisit this later, young man."

As she flounces out of the room, I jump on the computer and turn off the auto-complete preference. While I'm at it, I erase the entire search history. I can't believe I forgot to do this before—it must have been because Abby came in and interrupted me. I hope she doesn't pay any more visits for a while.

"Hi, Abby," Mom chirps as she opens the front door.

Oh crap. I absolutely do not want to talk to Abby. More importantly, I absolutely do not want to talk to Abby with Mom hanging around, so I scamper into the bathroom and lock the door. It's kind of a lame thing to do, but I can't make it to my bedroom without passing them on the way.

"Kevin, it's Abby … Kevin, where are you?"

I don't say a word. I'm invisible—I no longer exist.

"He's probably in the bathroom," says Abby.

"Are you in the bathroom, Kevin?"

"I'm sick," I moan.

"He's not sick. He's just hiding from me."

"Why are you hiding from Abby, honey?"

"I'm not hiding from Abby."

"He's hiding from me because he's a coward."

"I'm not a coward. I'm just sick." I stick my fingers down my throat and try to gag, but nothing happens. Geez, this is how half the girls at school spend their lunchtime. How difficult can it be?

"Please don't make yourself throw up," says Abby. "It's

kind of gross hearing you gag 'cause you're sticking your fingers down your throat."

"I'm not sticking my fingers down my throat."

"Of course you're not, honey. Now, why don't you come out and talk to Abby and me."

Hmmm, let me think about that. "No."

"Don't bother, Maggie," Abby says. "I only came around to ask Kevin why he wasn't at rehearsal today. I figured there'd be a simple explanation, but now I wonder if maybe there isn't something more complicated going on here. If there is, perhaps he can get it all out in the open before things get even uglier…Anyway, I should go. I'll let myself out. Goodbye, Kevin."

I hear her footsteps receding, but I'm too afraid to come out. Presumably Mom's still by the door, waiting to pounce.

"Kevin," Mom eventually whispers through the keyhole. "How would you feel about therapy?"

28

My new campaign to be invisible is failing miserably. I recited a litany of reasons why I wouldn't be able to make it to the baseball semifinal, but Brandon still dragged me along. He says it's the biggest game of the year so far—like I care—and there's bound to be some post-game action. And even though I don't want any action, I'm here anyway, loitering beside the Brookbank dugout, wearing dark clothing so I can't be seen. At least it's the top of the seventh inning already, and the way Spud's been pitching, the remainder of the game won't take long.

When the third of Brookbank's star batters strikes out, the opposition's cheerleaders surge forward and perform a short routine as part of the seventh-inning stretch. Then they ease back to the visitors' bench as Morgan and the other Brookbank cheerleaders take the field. They're almost through with their set when I realize that I'm actually watching the steps rather than ogling the girls. This is a first for me.

"And now Morgan Giddes, captain of Brookbank High's varsity cheerleading squad, will perform a solo dance she's created especially for the occasion," drones the announcer.

I figure I must have misheard him, but there's Morgan, standing apart from the cheerleaders, head raised high, waiting for the music to start.

And what music: modern, angular, with fiendish syncopated rhythms and a constantly fluctuating meter. I can't imagine a harder piece to choreograph to, but she clearly knows the music intimately. Every spike in the melody is reflected in her movements, every jarring chord provides the impetus for gestures both subtle and dynamic. It's part ballet, part interpretive dance, and completely, suicidally daring.

I'm suddenly reminded of the last time I saw Morgan dance: back in fifth grade during the infamous hobbies class. After I'd played "Dance of the Blessed Spirits," taking credit for the pianist's acrobatic performance, Morgan had danced ballet steps in the confined space beside the teacher's desk. Even when the CD got stuck she soldiered on, trusting the music she heard in her head, immersed in the beauty of her own performance rather than the sounds of stifled laughter from the kids in the class. She was so small back then, so fragile, but so much braver than I could ever be.

I look back at the field as Morgan sways in an imaginary breeze. So all these years she's continued to dance in private, avoiding the judgment that comes from opening up, being herself. I want to stand up and applaud her, but the first rumblings from the crowd aren't so appreciative. A few members of the opposing team have even begun laughing at her and pointing at Brandon—I guess they think he's still dating her.

Morgan doesn't seem to notice the intrusion, leaping from left to right and turning graceful circles on the spot. Meanwhile, a few of the cheerleaders have distanced themselves from her, creating a cushion in case the crowd turns against her any more.

Which they do. Most of the opposing team is now openly taunting her, and Brandon looks like he's getting mad. I figure it's only a matter of time before he says something back to them.

"Loser," he crows. I try to see who he's shouting at, and realize it's Morgan.

Hold on. *Morgan?*

"Give it up, freak," Brandon jeers, like he doesn't realize almost everyone present can hear him.

Morgan looks over suddenly, loses her balance, and crumples to the ground. Taylor rushes to her side and tries to help her up, but Morgan holds her ankle gingerly. As Brandon's insults compete with the frenetic music, I wonder if the grimace on Morgan's face has anything to do with her ankle.

Taylor tries to help her up again, but Morgan doesn't budge; she just stares at the ground, like the laughter rattling all around her is nothing more than she expected. I can see tears cascade down her cheeks, and when she finally gets up she does so alone. She looks straight ahead as she hobbles off the field. As soon as she rounds the bleachers, the music stops abruptly.

I look at Brandon, watching as the coach calls him over. He'll be thrown out of the game for sure now. He'll probably have to forgo the rest of the season for something like this.

"Now!" yells the coach. Brandon slopes over and stands before him, completely unrepentant.

"Listen up, Trent. Drop the commentary, okay? Remember, these are the semis. You've got more important things to think about than chicks."

This has to be a joke; he cannot seriously let Brandon off. I look at the rest of the team, watching to see if anybody else appears remotely outraged, but no one even seems to notice what's going on. Only Spud stares at Brandon, his eyes narrowed like he's trying not to pass gas.

Without thinking, I turn the corner and rush behind the bleachers, following Morgan. I crash into her almost immediately—she's leaning unsteadily against a metal support, trying to keep her weight off her ankle.

"I...I...I'm so sorry, Morgan. It was so wrong of Brandon to do that."

"Whatever." She wipes her eyes with the back of her hand.

"But it was disgraceful. He shouldn't be allowed to get away with saying stuff like that."

"Just go away."

"No, I won't go away. Something needs to be done. Aren't you going to do something?"

She lifts her eyes and glares at me. "Don't speak to me, Kevin. Don't you *dare* speak to me. You're the worst one of all."

"W-What? Why?"

"Because of that freakin' book you're compiling." She

grabs her breasts, shoves them upwards. "See these? Small, aren't they? And that's with a padded bra on... Are you getting all this? I don't want you to miss any of it. I'm an A cup, okay? So go ahead and write it." She starts to cry again.

"I'm not going to write it, Morgan," I say quietly.

"Why not? That's all you see, isn't it? A tight butt and small tits. A bunch of measurements, statistics."

"It's not like that."

"Bullshit. I know *exactly* what it's like. As long as I prance around half naked, everything's cool. As long as I let Brandon touch me any way he wants, everything's cool. As long as I pretend not to notice boys ogling me, everything's cool. But as soon as I say I've had enough, I'm frigid. And when I dance the way I want to, I'm taunted." She stares off into the distance. "Why is it so wrong for me to be myself?"

"It's not wrong. That was a beautiful dance, Morgan... reminded me of fifth grade—"

"When I should've learned my lesson," she chokes.

"No. This is isn't your fault. Brandon shouldn't have said those things."

"Stop it, Kevin. Just stop it, okay? You want me to believe you actually give a crap about what Brandon says to me, but you're just the same as him... and I guess I figured you were different. All of us thought you were different."

A collective gasp draws our attention, back through gaps in the bleachers to the field of play. The ball flies through the air momentarily, then Brandon makes a diving catch and unleashes a bullet throw to first base, where the runner is tagged out before he can get back—a double play. Inning over. The crowd cheers. His teammates mob him.

Morgan takes a deep breath and grits her teeth. Her jawbones flex. "If you want to help—if you *really* want to help—then explain something to me: how come Brandon Trent gets to hurt me, abuse me, and humiliate me, but I'm the one hiding behind the bleachers while everybody chants his name?"

She doesn't wait for a reply, but hobbles off in the direction of the parking lot, confused and hopelessly alone.

As soon as she's gone it occurs to me that she desperately needed a hug, but I was too slow to react. Then again, why should I get to hug her and tell her it's all going to be okay, when I'm the reason it's not?

29

Ms. Kowalski appears flustered, which is a new look for her. She has a standard repertoire of facial expressions—exhausted, bemused, incensed—but she rarely looks flustered.

"Kevin, I'd like a word with you. In private."

The class looks up in unison, stares at her momentarily, then shifts its attention to me. I feel a dozen pairs of eyes boring into me as I climb out of my chair and follow her into the corridor.

Ominously, she closes the door to give us some privacy.

"Kevin, I just want you to know that I haven't said a word to your mother about your connection to the Graduation Rituals."

"Okay."

"I know you're aware that I don't approve of them, and I'm disappointed that you of all students would be involved.

But I've made it a point not to come between you and your mother."

"Okay."

"Okay. Good. I just wanted to make that clear before she finds out about your involvement."

"Ok—" Hold on. "Finds out? What do you mean, finds out?"

"Well, Zach Thomas requested permission to join your mom's class, and knowing him, he's not doing it to show his support for the senior girls."

"But s-surely you didn't let him in?"

"Of course. We had to," she says breezily. "It's school policy that no student be denied access to a course on the basis of gender. He could sue us."

"But it's not even a real course!"

"Kevin, that's just the attitude toward Women's Studies that your mother is trying to undo—"

"No, no. I mean, she's not teaching it for credit."

"But she's teaching it on school grounds, so she's bound by the same rules as any other teacher."

Oh crap. This is really bad.

"Can I have permission to join the Women's Studies class, please?" I ask.

"What? Why?"

"Because I have to stop him."

"Not a good enough reason." Ms. K shakes her head vigorously. "Not good enough at all."

"Um, how about: because I know I've been a jerk, and I want to make amends?"

She hesitates, and stares at me like she's trying to gauge my sincerity. "Okay," she says finally. "Permission granted."

I rush back into class, grab my bag, and less than a minute later I'm standing outside the door of my mom's classroom. I'm about to walk in when I hear Morgan's voice rise above the general murmur:

"Well, *I'm* not comfortable with him being here. Have you all forgotten he's part of the problem?"

I peek through the small window in the door and see that her comments are aimed at Zach, who doesn't look perturbed at all. He's leaning back in his chair, a look of utter contentment on his face.

"Now, Morgan," says Mom soothingly. "I hear your concerns, but let's not play the blame game until we've given Zach a chance to speak."

"But he's involved in the Book of Busts, for Christ's sake!"

"The Book of Busts?"

"Yeah. It's where the boys write down the measurements of all the girls in the senior year and publish the results."

"That's a horrible accusation to make, Morgan," trills Mom, turning violently red. "That any boy would dare to undertake such a despicable and degrading exercise is unfathomable. Zach, tell me this isn't true. Tell me this book is a myth."

Zach looks suddenly and convincingly contrite. "I'm so sorry," he mumbles, "but it's true. That's why I'm here. I know what I did was wrong, and I feel *terrible*."

"Well, I must say," fizzes Mom, like a bomb craving detonation, "you've either got a lot of guts or a lot of nerve to come in here today, given your involvement in something as egregious as this."

I don't think Zach knows what "egregious" means—he looks confused—but in the context he knows it isn't good, so he hangs his head like a shamed puppy and fiddles with his hands.

"You're right," he sighs. "But I haven't really done anything with the book—"

"But you would've done if you could," Morgan shoots back. "I bet you wanted the job of compiling the book. Then all the girls would've been lining up dates with you instead."

"Morgan!" protests Mom. "What on earth are you saying? You're not seriously suggesting that girls arranged dates with the boy compiling this book, are you?"

Morgan looks away. "Yes."

"But why?"

"So they could give him inflated measurements ... boost their scores a little."

Mom's face has morphed from a scarlet red to a pale, almost ghostly white. "Has anyone here done such a thing?"

One by one, Jessica, Kayla, and Taylor raise their hands.

"B-B-But how can you think a boy like that is worthy of even a second of your time?" chokes Mom. "Why wouldn't you just tell him to crawl back to his cave?"

"I pretty much did," laughs Taylor. "I told him he was a loser who ought to know better."

"Well, that's something, I suppose."

"Oh, come on," says Morgan quietly. "Let's just be honest for once ... almost all of us are responsible for this. None of us wanted to rock the boat. No one was willing to stand up to the boys and say the Graduation Rituals suck. We just played along like every other senior class before us, because it beats being called boring or frigid. We could've stuck together and ended it ... We *should've* stuck together. We shouldn't have let it go on."

The room is suddenly silent. Everyone seems to be studying the floor.

"I don't know what we were thinking." Kayla nods solemnly. "He's not even that attractive," she adds, provoking laughter all around.

"But that's not relevant, is it, Kayla," Mom chastens her. "One of the purposes of our class is to move beyond people as objects, and that goes for boys too. It's his behavior and his attitude toward others that defines a man, not his looks. The boy you're talking about is a discredit to all males because of his blatant disrespect toward women."

I notice that Zach is laughing now, and everyone seems to have forgotten that he's in the doghouse too. Everyone except Mom.

"I'm surprised to see you laughing, Zach," she chides. "After all, he's one of your friends."

"No, not him. Like Kayla says, he's a complete tool, and he's pretty freakin' weird, and his name—"

"He's not weird, and he's not a tool," shouts Abby suddenly, interrupting Zach before he can say my name.

Thank you, Abby. Thank you.

"Oh, whatever," drones Zach. "Just 'cause you want him doesn't mean he's not a loser. Just ask any of the girls who went out on dates with Ke—"

"He's a really decent guy if you'd only bother to see past this stupid book," Abby practically screams, drowning out Zach's voice. "It's tearing us apart, all of us. This isn't just about one boy, it's about all the boys who join in these pathetic Graduation Rituals...including Zach."

She's staring at him with a blinding intensity, daring him to utter another word. I know that stare, and so I know why Zach's having second thoughts about saying my name. Right now, I love Abby with all my heart.

"But I'm not compiling it," complains Zach, then hesitates as Abby unleashes another withering look. He takes a deep breath. "Kevin Mopsely is."

At once, I feel cold and nauseous. Mom seems frozen to the spot, jaw hanging open and shoulders slumped. Across the room from her, Zach smiles broadly, looking around like he's expecting congratulations for having outed me. I don't know how he knows we're related, but I never did get around to checking the Web page for Mom's class. Maybe Zach was a little more disciplined, a little more motivated—he always said he was onto me. I guess he decided now was the time to bring my world crashing down.

Mom doesn't say anything for almost a minute, so some of the girls begin asking her if she's okay.

"She's okay," says Abby, wiping away a stray tear. "She just needs a moment, that's all."

"Yeah," mutters Zach. "She's just discovered her son is compiling the Book of Busts—"

And suddenly the room is filled with shouting and crying and I know I have to walk in and take the heat. I have to face my mom. I have to stand at the front of the class like a man and let GRRLS hurl insults at me. It's no more than I deserve.

I place my hand firmly on the door handle, press down—then sprint straight out of the school.

30

On the way home I formulate a plan, which doesn't take long as there's only one course of action left: I need to hand over the Book of Busts to someone else in such a way that the guys won't hate me or beat the crap out of me. Right now I'm running low on the popularity meter—I've lost my quartet friends, and it's pretty clear that all the senior girls hate me—and I'm counting on the guys to make sure I reach graduation with all my limbs intact. After all, there may be multiple groups currently planning retribution.

When I get home, I lock myself in my room and wait for Mom. I figure I'll know when she arrives because she'll try to break my door down.

An hour passes, then two. Eventually I hear the front door click open downstairs and Matt the Mutt greets Mom like she's the center of the universe—which, at least for the dog, she probably is.

I wait for her to climb the stairs, but she doesn't. I wait for her to scream, but she doesn't. There's not a sound down there. It's the quietest our house has ever been.

I let another five minutes go by, but by then I can't bear the suspense any longer. I want to get this over with. There's no way to avoid it, so the best thing is if she just reams me, grounds me, tells me I'm evil and disowns or castrates me, exactly as Abby predicted.

I tiptoe down the stairs and peek into the kitchen, and the living room, and the study. She's not there. And then I notice that her bedroom door is closed, so I creep over and knock as gently as I can.

There's no answer, but I detect the faintest hint of moaning from the other side, so I knock again. Still nothing, but I open the door anyway.

She's sitting against the wall, hugging her knees like she's twelve years old. I think I've heard her say that developmental regression is sometimes a result of an emotionally devastating event, which I guess puts the blame firmly on me.

"Are you okay, Mom?"

"Why why why why why—"

"Mo-om?"

Her mouth continues to open and close, but she's stuck on *why* like a damaged CD.

I take a tentative step toward her, then another. "Mom, I'm really sorry."

She sighs. "Where did I go wrong? What was it I failed to do? . . . failed to explain?"

"Nothing. You didn't fail at all."

"Why were you at Hooters?"

Hooters? Oh, the credit card statement must have come. Crap.

"That was when I was with Dad."

"What were you and your father doing at Hooters?"

I should tell her the truth—Dad was getting hammered and ogling the waitresses—but I think it would break her heart, so I don't say a word.

A moment later she's crying, and although Dad used to have her in tears at least once a month, it's the first time in my life I've been responsible. And I don't feel glib or defiant or even defensive anymore. I just feel like an asshole.

"I'm sorry, Mom. I really am. I just wanted to be popular for a change."

"Popular with whom? I mean, it doesn't seem like you're popular with the girls in my class."

"No. It hasn't exactly worked out like I planned."

"You *planned* this?" A fresh dose of crying ensues, and she peers up at me through the curtain of tears. "Who are you?"

"I'm me. Kevin."

"No, you can't be. My Kevin would never do something so hurtful." She closes her eyes. "I think you should go stay with your father this weekend. I can't have you around right now."

I crouch down beside her. "I don't think he's going to be very helpful, Mom. I really don't want to go—"

"I don't care. *I* need you out of here, and I think that spending some time with your father will help."

The idea is so stupid that I snort, hoping she'll take offense and have it out with me right here, right now. But she doesn't bite. She just remains crumpled against the wall, gently rocking back and forth.

"There's money in the drawer. Call your father, then call a cab. I expect you gone in half an hour. If you can't figure things out by talking to him, then don't bother coming back."

She doesn't look up, so after a few more seconds of silence I prepare to leave. I can't believe it, but Abby was right: Mom's disowned me. Then again, so has Abby, and Morgan and Taylor and Kayla and Jessica, and Nathan and probably even Caitlin. And I'm still not clear on how everything got so incredibly messed up.

I pause at the doorway and listen to the awful sobbing that became the soundtrack of our lives after Dad left. Mom cried for so long I began to wonder if she'd ever stop. But these last few weeks, since she started teaching at Brookbank High, there haven't been any tears. She's even begun to resemble that bohemian scholar in the photo upstairs: determined, energetic, content. My insanely dysfunctional high school—the bane of my existence—gave her a taste of happiness, of fulfillment. And she really did make a difference. Had I undone everything?

I look over my shoulder, but I can't bear to make eye contact. "Mom, I know I don't deserve it, but would you apologize to your class for me? I mean, for everything I've done."

She shakes her head. "No, Kevin, I won't … They took a vote. They don't want me to come back."

31

Dad's not exactly thrilled to see me. He pretends to be engrossed in an NBA playoff game when I arrive, and as soon as it ends he channel surfs until he finds another game that's just starting.

"Dad, can we talk?"

He sighs and grabs a beer from the crate beside the sofa. The crate's full, so I guess he just keeps replenishing the supply whenever it dwindles. He cracks open the beer and hands it to me.

"No thanks," I say. "I don't want any tonight."

Dad looks hurt. "It was good enough for you last time."

"I know. I just… need to think straight."

"I see. So you're saying that because I drink beer, I don't think straight, is that it?"

"No, that's not what I'm saying."

"Isn't it?"

"No. I just need to keep a clear head. I've had a crappy week, okay?"

"Okay." Dad finally switches off the TV and turns to face me. "So what's the problem?"

"Remember I said I'd been on a couple of dates?" Dad nods and a trickle of beer oozes out of the corner of his mouth, but he doesn't seem to notice. "Well, I went on a couple more, also with different girls—"

"Hell yeah!" He's suddenly pumped up. "My son the player." He proffers his fist, inviting me to bash knuckles in a Brandonesque gesture of affection. He doesn't seem to notice my halfhearted response.

"Yeah, but ... I mean, the point is I wasn't exactly interested in a relationship. I think I ... well, I just wanted to hook up with them because, you know, they're popular and cute."

"That's great. You're totally following the advice I gave you last time—just hook up with the hot ones and move on."

He's right about one thing—this is the same stuff he said before, and back then it felt liberating to be able to open up, to feel unjudged and wholly supported. Only now it doesn't, and I don't think it's just because I'm sober.

"No, Dad. I don't think you're getting it." I sit up straighter, which is hard because the sofa is soft and mushy. "The point is ... well, what I'm trying to say is I, you know, *used* those girls." I take a deep breath. "See, it's all because of the Book of Busts, the thing that I was supposed to compile this year for the Rituals."

Dad looks confused.

195

"The Book of Busts is this book where we write down the measurements of all the girls in the senior class."

Dad resumes his proud-parent-of-an-honor-student expression.

"And, well, the thing is, some of the sexiest girls went out on dates with me just so they could fake their numbers."

"Uh-huh," Dad grunts, completely unmoved by my confession.

"I guess what I'm trying to say is, they weren't interested in me—they were just interested in, you know, inflating their bust size. And even though I suppose I kind of knew deep down they didn't exactly, um...like me, I hooked up with them anyway just 'cause they're hot. See? I used them, and they used me."

"So everybody used everybody else," summarizes Dad approvingly. "Sounds like you all got what you wanted."

"B-But that's not the point, is it?"

Dad sighs and stares off into space. He's clearly getting bored. "Then why don't you tell me what the point is, Kevin."

"The point is...well, the point is that while I was fixated on getting to second base, they were hating me for it. I even messed things up with Abby...the one girl who liked me for who I am, and I had to go check out her bra size like it mattered somehow."

"Hey, don't underestimate tits, son. Tits are important."

"What?"

"Just kidding." Dad snorts and slaps his thigh. "But you

really need to stop making such a big deal of all this. No harm, no foul, you know?"

I can't believe we're having this conversation. It's like we've undergone a weird role reversal, with me as responsible middle-aged father and Dad as sex-starved teenage son.

"Have you been listening? What I did was wrong, don't you see that?"

He clearly hasn't seen that.

"Dad, I even went out with one girl who had just stopped dating a guy I know. I mean, it's not exactly like I'm friends with the guy, but I wasn't even sure they *had* stopped dating. And that made me want her even more. You have to admit, that's messed up."

Dad's smiling broadly, like we're finally discussing a subject on which he can offer real guidance. "You're just analyzing this too much. It's not that complicated. If you want something, and she wants something, then just do it." He narrows his eyes. "You're eighteen now, Kevin. You're an adult. Consenting adults can do whatever the hell they want. Period. And if other people don't like it, they can go screw themselves."

I roll my eyes. "Can you just be serious for once?"

He frowns. "I am being serious."

I wait for him to laugh, but he doesn't. "You're kidding, right?" I wait again. "You have to be kidding." Okay, so he's not kidding. "I said I was kind of hoping this girl was still involved with the guy—that it would make me want her even more. Are you even listening to me? I'm saying I liked the thought of helping her cheat on him. What does that make me?"

"It makes you human," he sighs. "It makes you a guy. What else do you want me to say?"

"I want you to say...I don't know what I want you to say! That I'm an asshole or something. I want you to say you have the first clue what I'm talking about...that I was wrong to go after someone who's already involved in another relationship—"

"You mean, like I did?"

I actually wasn't thinking about him, so I hesitate before answering. "Well, yeah, I guess you did."

Dad downs the rest of his beer. "So that's what all this is about, huh? That's why you're here. You want me to apologize."

"No, this isn't about you. It's about me."

"Is it really, Kevin? Seems as if this is absolutely about me. The way you've come here tonight even though I'm really busy, didn't give me any choice in the matter, all so you can start lecturing me about infidelity." Dad crushes his empty can in a threateningly masculine way. "Must be nice to see things in black and white, but it's not always that simple."

I can't believe he's managed to turn this around so it's about him. Suddenly all the thoughts I've concealed for the past eight months come bubbling to the surface, and I don't feel like sparing his feelings anymore.

"I did *not* come here to lecture you. But now that you mention it, I do think infidelity is pretty black and white, actually. I mean, you either decide to make it happen or you decide not to make it happen, right? No one forced you to shack up with Kimberly."

Dad just shakes his head like I'm too naive to know any better. "Geez, you're just like your mom ... always were."

"Right now, that sounds a whole lot better than the alternative."

"You have no idea what you're talking about. I was sick of being judged, sick of apologizing for the way I felt. And after twenty-some years I'd had enough of listening to her spout that feminist crap all the time."

"She was doing that when you met. If you found it so repulsive, why didn't you say something about it then? If you ask me, you're just looking for an excuse to justify the fact that you're an even bigger asshole than me."

To my surprise, Dad just laughs. "You're losers, both of you."

"*Us?* You think *we're* losers?" I can feel my hands clenching into fists, heart pounding like I'm running for my life. "When did you figure that out, huh? While you were getting hammered? Or while you were watching TV in this shithole of an apartment? No, Dad, *you're* the loser ... And you know what? I think you know it too."

"Don't pretend you're any different—"

"But I *am* different. Thirty years from now I won't be living like this. And I won't be getting my kicks at Hooters, either ... dropping fifty bucks to ogle waitresses who are too polite to admit you gross them out."

I can tell he wants to hit me really badly, but he doesn't. He just gets up off the sofa and walks over to the front door, then opens it so I can leave. Dismissed by both parents in the same evening—what are the chances?

I look at him as I walk through the door, noticing, more

than ever before, the deep wrinkles on his forehead and the poorly dyed black hair combed across his bald patch. He's trying to look intimidating, but he's so pudgy around the edges that the impression falls flat. I might be wrong, but his defiance seems desperate ... like I've just held up a mirror to the reality of his existence, and he can't bear to face the reflection.

32

I've got enough money left to take a taxi home, but I need to walk. It takes me over three hours, through parts of town I wouldn't normally cross, but it gives me time to think. And even though it's chilly, I feel fine. As each mile passes, I sense the distance between my dad and me growing. It feels good. It feels cathartic.

I think about Natasha in fifth grade, the way she couldn't look me in the eye when she asked me to teach her the flute. I've never thought about this before, but it was clearly a big deal for her to ask, and I made a joke out of it. I said what Brandon would say, only I'm not Brandon. I've never been Brandon. I never will be Brandon. And that's a good thing.

And then there's Abby. I can still picture her lying beside me on the bed, her head resting against the palm of her hand. She was topless, but there was no hint of embarrassment because she was with me, and she loved me. I remember her smile, the softness of her skin, the scent of her hair, and the way she held me like I was the only person in the universe who mattered.

I try to impose a different ending on the evening, but the fact remains—I looked at her bra. I didn't have to. There was no reason to. But I did. Why? I'd never been interested in her bra size before, and I'm fairly certain I wouldn't have added it to the book even if she hadn't caught me. I just did it because . . . well, because I could. Because I felt entitled to. Something so personal, so emotionally charged, yet I acted like it was my business, my right to see into every aspect of her life, to claim every part of her . . . whether she wanted me to or not.

She said I treated her like an object. And as I feel the tears running down my face, I hate myself more than ever before, because I know that she was horribly, painfully right.

I was an asshole.

What am I now?

When I finally turn onto our street, I can see a faint glow in the window of Mom's bedroom. I don't want to go in if she's still up. Then I see a light in Abby's bedroom window as well, and without thinking I pull out my cell phone and call her.

"Why are you calling me in the middle of the night?" Abby whispers angrily across the line.

"Because I need to talk."

"To me?"

"To someone I trust."

"Then why don't you call Brandon?"

I deserve that, I know I do, but it still hurts.

"Please, Abby. Mom threw me out earlier, so I went to stay with Dad. Then he threw me out. I've got nowhere left to go."

"Well, you're not coming here." She pauses. "Where are you?"

"Just outside your house. By the tree."

She sighs. "Okay, wait there. I'll be down in a minute."

She hangs up and appears moments later carrying a couple of blankets. In silence she sits beside me, draping one blanket across my shoulders and wrapping the other around herself. I'm grateful for it; now that I'm no longer walking, the air feels suddenly colder.

"So I know why your mom wanted to kick you out," she says softly. "But what's the story with your dad?"

"We had an argument about everything that's happened."

"Everything that's happened to you, or everything that's happened to him?"

"Both."

"Oh. And what did you argue about?"

"I said I've been acting like a jerk, and Dad got all 'screw everyone' on me. So then I said he's been a jerk too, and he kicked me out. God, it was like talking to a middle-aged version of Brandon, or ... "

Abby looks at me for the first time. "Or what?" she presses.

I look up at the moonlit leaves dancing in the breeze. "Or maybe it felt so weird 'cause it was like looking into the future and seeing what *I* might become." I take a deep breath and puff out my cheeks, which feels oddly therapeutic. "I didn't believe Mom when she said it would be helpful for me to talk to him, but I guess she was right. I've been such an asshole, Abby. I'm still an asshole."

Abby shakes her head, hair flying loosely from side to side. "No, you're not. Assholes take pride in their own stupidity, and I don't see you having much fun right now. Yesterday you were an asshole, but today...well, it's up to you. You're not a lost cause, Kevin."

Is she really forgiving me for the things I've said and done? I meet her gaze, trying to divine an answer, but her face is implacable. I want to tell her how much I need everything to be right again between us, but where to begin? I've held myself together pretty well, but now I can feel a tear escaping again, and another. Abby kindly averts her eyes.

"Kevin, I know you think I don't understand what you've been going through the last few weeks, but you're wrong. Don't you think I've wondered what it would be like to be really popular? What it would be like to be told I'm sexy? But what's the point, right? At the end of the day, I'm still me. And if that's not good enough, then too bad, because, well...personally, I think I'm pretty damn cool."

She smiles, and I can feel the tension in my chest lessen a bit. I dab my eyes quickly. "You're popular, you know. And for what it's worth, I think you're sexy too."

She nods. "Ditto."

A silence descends on us, but it's not entirely comfortable. Abby plucks individual blades of grass and holds them up to the moon, taking in the beauty of the night, but she won't look at me. The healing process may have begun, but we're still a long way from the carefree intimacy we used to share.

"What are you going to do?" she says finally.

"I don't know."

"Hmmm. Well, just remember that senior year isn't over yet. You still have time to make things right."

She removes the blanket from her shoulders and hands it to me. I can still feel the warmth from her body in the fibers. She squeezes my arm gently and stands up, and seconds later she's gone and I'm alone, sitting on the grass beneath a tree in the middle of the night, wishing I could just turn back the clock.

33

School's over for the day, and I'm hiding behind the trees that border the student parking lot. It's a risky place to be—any number of things could happen to me out here. I could get in trouble for loitering; I could get lynched by GRRLS; I could witness freshmen making out. But I wait anyway, because I need to talk to Morgan, and I need to talk to her alone.

By four o'clock almost every car in the lot has gone, but Morgan still hasn't appeared. Her white Miata is parked in the space nearest the school entrance, because she's always the first to arrive in the morning. No wonder even the teachers love her.

Eventually she emerges and sashays over to her car. She's smiling, as usual, and suddenly I find this very admirable. I mean, just last week Brandon publicly humiliated her and her friends turned their backs on her. If anyone ought to patrol the corridors with a scowl etched on her face, it's Morgan.

"Hey, Morgan," I say, mirroring her smile.

"Huh?" She looks over at me as I push the last branch out of the way. "Oh God, it's you, Kevin. Stay away, I've got Mace."

"No, it's cool," I say without thinking, maybe because that's what I've heard Brandon say when guys threaten him for hooking up with their girlfriends.

"No, Kevin, it's not cool. It's so totally not cool."

"Oh." This never happens to Brandon. "Okay."

Morgan unlocks her car and is about to climb in when she glances at me. I think my slumped shoulders are weakening her resistance.

"Just one question," she says, leaning against the car door. "Was it worth it?"

I hesitate. "Honestly?"

"Honestly."

I look away. "I guess I liked being popular, you know? I liked being noticed. But now the people I care about the most hate me, so ... no," I say emphatically. "It wasn't worth it."

"Are you just saying that because you got caught?"

"Well, it doesn't exactly help any."

To my surprise, Morgan laughs. "What the hell were you thinking? I know these Graduation Rituals have been going on for years, but this year your mom was teaching a *Women's Studies* course. You must have realized that was going to change everything."

"I didn't know she was teaching it until I'd agreed to do

the book. I guess I just hoped she wouldn't find out about it."

Morgan laughs even harder. "Are you serious? She's your mom. How could you possibly think she wouldn't find out?"

I just shake my head, because there's really nothing to say. When I look up again, Morgan looks more serious.

"What is it you want to say to me, Kevin? Why are you here?"

I take a deep breath and tell her what I've been thinking about all weekend—my Grand Plan. It's complicated, and I know she's reluctant to help me after everything I've done, but I'm hoping that the chance to get back at Brandon is too much for her to resist.

She spends a few minutes pulling a variety of indecisive faces, but finally settles on a smile that tells me she's willing to play her part. And for the first time in weeks I feel proud of myself. Not cool. Not popular. Just proud.

"Do you need a ride home?" she asks, sinking into the leather bucket seat.

"Sure."

I clamber in and she pulls away slowly, checking her mirrors and signaling like a law-abiding adult. If she weren't so beautiful, Morgan would have to be considered one of the dorkiest girls in school.

"Have you and Abby ever dated?" she asks.

"No."

"Why not?"

"Um … it's just never happened. What about you and Brandon? How did that happen?"

Morgan groans. "He was the first boy to ask me out since freshman year. I guess I just wanted to have a date again."

I take a quick peek to see if she's kidding, but she doesn't seem to be.

"But that's impossible. Every guy at Brookbank wants to date you."

"That's kind of you to say, but it doesn't change the fact that before Brandon, no one had asked me out in three years. I think I just wanted to feel ... wanted. And Brandon's so popular and everything. I got suckered in, I guess."

"So who are you going to prom with?"

"I'm not going with anyone. Today, all of the girls from the Women's Studies class decided to go solo. With everything that's happened the past few weeks, we figure it'll make things less stressful in the long run."

I can't help smiling. "That'll make my mom proud. She really loved teaching you. She said you were the best students she's had in years."

"Yeah?" Morgan is obviously touched. She takes a deep breath. "I wish we hadn't told her to leave. It was all kind of heat-of-the-moment, you know? Do you reckon she'd come back if we asked?"

"No, I don't think so. Not because of me ... just because she's already achieved what she set out to do. Like, you're all standing up for each other now, and before long Brandon and his posse won't know what hit them. I think she'd say that's a job well done."

Morgan laughs again, a soft, gentle laugh that warms me from the inside out. "I like the sound of that," she says.

She follows my directions and soon I'm home. She puts the car in park and pulls up the hand brake, then turns to face me.

"Abby was right about you. You're not such a bad guy after all."

It's not quite the compliment I was hoping for, but when Morgan leans over and tries to kiss me on the cheek, I *pull away.*

"Whoa!" she exclaims. "What was that for? I was just giving you a friendly peck on the cheek. It's not like I was trying to French kiss you or anything!"

I can feel my cheeks burning red. "I know. I mean ... I'm sorry. I don't know why I did that."

She stares out her window crossly, so I undo the seat belt and open my car door. And that's when it hits me.

"Actually, I do know why I pulled away."

"Oh yeah, why's that?"

"Because that's Abby's house." I point next door. "And I think I'm ... I think I—"

"It's okay." Morgan is smiling again. "I get it."

"You do?"

"Yeah. And for what it's worth, I'm glad you're back to being you again."

I can't believe what I'm hearing. "But I always figured you thought I was a total geek."

"Yeah, of course. But that doesn't mean I didn't admire you, or find you interesting. It just means that unlike Brandon, you've got a functioning brain cell." She laughs again at the look on my face. "Maybe you need to work on embracing your geekiness."

I climb out. Morgan pulls away, and I'm left standing on the sidewalk. It's sunny and warm, and I feel unbelievably contented. Not only is Morgan Giddes my new friend, but I think I'm ... I think I ...

34

Now don't forget, baseball final's this Thursday at seven," says Brandon, pacing along the gap between the tables. "I expect all of you to be there."

Everyone cheers, but the sound is rather pathetic on account of the fact that there are only eleven guys left. I realize that they're all members of the baseball team, with the exception of me.

"You got that, Kevin?" Brandon looks directly at me, apparently coming to the same realization himself.

"Yeah, wouldn't miss it for anything," I say truthfully.

"Cool. So before we get onto the Book of Busts, I have to ask why the hell the Strategic Graffiti Campaign is still so far behind schedule. Anybody got an excuse?"

"'Cause no one's doing it except you and me," Zach grumbles, with an impressively pouty lower lip.

Brandon shakes his head disappointedly. "Well, that's going to change."

Zach pulls out a few pieces of paper and hands one to each of us, along with a thick-nibbed Sharpie. I study the paper, which contains a series of inspired one-liners like "Kayla is a transvestite" and "Morgan is a frigid slut." Apparently Zach isn't completely clear on oxymorons.

"So," Brandon continues, "we're all going to take these sheets and visit the girls' bathrooms. Then we're going to write these little quotes on every available inch of wall space. Got it?"

He looks around, waiting for us to indicate that we share his unbridled enthusiasm for the project. He clearly doesn't like what he sees, because he throws the remaining pieces of paper (I guess Zach thought more guys would show up) on the table in front of him and raises his fist aggressively.

"It's time, guys. If we don't pull together now, what are we? We're pussies, that's what."

"Damn right," adds Zach eloquently.

"Look, I'm not being unreasonable here," Brandon insists, wringing his hands for effect. "Remember, we didn't declare war on the girls—they declared war on us. And I don't see any Brookbank professors showing up to teach a course on Men's Studies—no offense, Kevin. So now it's our turn to strike back." He and Zach exchange a meaningful glance, then look straight at me. "Kevin, you can start us off by writing the first few quotes."

So here it is, my moment of reckoning. I take a deep breath.

"Um, no thanks. I don't think so."

Brandon knows I must be joking, so he gives me a few seconds to laugh or change my mind. Then another few seconds.

"You're kidding, right?"

"No."

"What the f—"

"You see, Brandon, I don't think this is really the most productive use of our time. In fact, I don't think any of the things we do represent a useful investment of our energies. So I'd like to propose an alternative plan."

"And what's that?"

"We disband immediately."

Brandon lets rip a half-crazed laugh. "Now I *know* you're screwing with me."

"No, Brandon, I'm not."

He hesitates, narrows his eyes. "Don't mess this up, Mopsely. You were nothing before you joined us, but I made you popular, made you *somebody*. If you walk away now, you'll never have it this good again."

Even though I'm gripped by fear, I can still see the humor in a comment so far out of whack with reality.

"What's good about this, huh, Brandon? Everyone hates us, and it's easy to see why. Look at us... discussing girls behind their backs, scribbling insults on the walls of their bathrooms when they're not looking, getting their measurements like the numbers somehow mean something. Is this really the best we can do? Don't we have just a little more pride than that?"

No one interrupts my speech, and I let the silence linger. I can almost feel some of the guys coming around, but then Brandon storms to the back of the room and stabs his finger repeatedly against a poster advertising Brookbank's upcoming ten-year reunion.

"You want pride? This is pride," he mutters menacingly. "Coming back in ten years' time, knowing we accomplished something. You can disappear if you want, but *we* won't fade away. We'll matter then, because we matter now."

"That's what this is about? Our ten-year reunion?"

"This is the forty-third year of the Graduation Rituals, Mopsely. For forty-two years no one had a problem, but all of a sudden your mom comes in and tradition goes to hell."

"Of course the girls had a problem with the Rituals. They were just too frightened to complain, that's all. And that doesn't mean everything was okay. It just means we've taken forty-three years too many to shut this thing down."

Brandon slams his fist against a table. "You're not shutting anything down."

It's weird, but there's still a part of me that wants to save Brandon from himself, even though I know deep down he's a lost cause. I lean forward.

"Come on, Brandon," I whisper earnestly. "Let's end this our way."

"*Our* way? Who the hell do you think you are?" He smiles like my impertinence is comical. "I can't believe I was ever stupid enough to put you in charge of the book. Well, congratulations. You've officially regained loser status."

"I don't think so," I reply calmly. "No, I think you're the loser unless you end this."

"Oh, yeah? Well, if I'm such a loser, how come I got to make out with Morgan Giddes while you can't even get with an ugly bitch like Abby White?"

I feel the flash of white-hot anger. A part of me wants to jump Brandon, even though I know he'll beat the crap out of me. A part of me wants to scream that I *have* gotten with Abby, and that Morgan tried to kiss *me*, even though she ditched Brandon when she caught him stealing second. But to my credit, I don't say any of these things. Because this isn't about Abby, or Morgan, or even Brandon—it's about me. And I'm not here to outdo Brandon. I'm here to undo him.

"Come on, Brandon. It's over. You know it is. Look around you ... the only guys left are your teammates. Even the football players who flunked remedial algebra had the sense to get out. Let's end this with some dignity."

Brandon erupts in laughter again, but I can tell he's forcing it now. "Screw dignity, and screw you. You want to go, then go. Just give us the book on your way out."

"Can't do that ... I set fire to it."

Zach leaps out of his seat. "Bullshit. You wouldn't have the guts."

Interesting.

"Okay," I say. "It's in my locker."

"Well then," Zach hisses, no doubt enjoying his renewed status as Brandon's undisputed right-hand man, "you've got five minutes to go get it or you'll be dreaming about prom from a hospital bed."

I can't believe Zach just said something as melodramatic as that—it's really not cool—but maybe he actually means it. To be honest, I'm a little surprised that my performance hasn't yet warranted at least a minor beating, and I don't plan on hanging around long enough for that to change.

"Hold on—Spud!" shouts Brandon, ushering over the

human cannonball. "Go with him. Make sure he doesn't try anything."

Spud obediently falls in step behind me. I really want to get out now, but I can't help taking one last look around the mostly empty room. I expect to see Brandon's grimace on every face, so I'm taken aback at the sight of his teammates. Gone is the swagger, the untouchable self-confidence; they now have the downtrodden appearance of a bedraggled platoon following their leader on one final, hopeless mission. I look back at Brandon, and I know immediately he's seen it too.

"I wish you could just admit you were wrong," I say, breaking the silence. "The girls would worship you for it, you know ... And what are you getting out of this stuff anyway? You think every girl in school figures she owes you something? Are you getting a kick out of being in control?"

Brandon doesn't answer, and he doesn't move—he just stands beside the poster, like that's all the evidence he needs. It's a predictable poster, too: smiling twenty-somethings reliving the glory days of high school. And that's when the truth finally dawns on me.

"Are you afraid, Brandon? That every girl here will forget about you the moment senior year is over? Is that what this is about?"

Brandon rolls his eyes, but when he opens his mouth, nothing comes out. Suddenly I have a vision of him in Hooters thirty years from now, professing his adoration for a waitress half his age as neighboring tables jeer him. I have to concentrate to keep the corners of my mouth from twitching into a smile.

"Look, Brandon, I hate to break it to you, but you better hope they *do* forget about you. Because at our ten-year reunion, the ones who remember you won't be looking back on the good ol' days...they'll just be wondering how on earth you ever made them care."

As Spud and I walk out, I can already hear a hushed murmur behind me, and I know that Brandon will be doing everything in his power to keep the Rituals going. Maybe it's because he can't let a dork like Kevin Mopsely derail any project he masterminds, or maybe it's because I've seen his glaring weakness: Brookbank's star jock has already reached his prime, and it's all downhill from here.

"Listen, Spud," I say, knowing what's about to happen and wanting to spare him the humiliation, "you may not want to come with me. 'Cause I'm not giving the book to Brandon, I'm just not. And things are about to get crazy."

Spud arches an eyebrow theatrically. "Things are already crazy."

Whoa! Spud Beasley just *spoke*.

"You just...spoke," I gasp, even though that's quite a rude thing to say.

"Of course I spoke. You think that 'Dude, like, whoa' stuff is all I've got? I just do that because it's my role, you know? Tough guy, man of few words, speaks with his fists, that sort of thing. I just figured it would simplify my interactions with peers if I presented a consistent and coherent persona. You understand?"

"Whoa."

"Thing is, I was going to come with you anyway. What you said back there, it's true. It's time to close shop on this stuff."

"B-But... you're the editor of the Alternative Yearbook."

Spud grins sheepishly. "Yeah, another book that Brandon won't be getting his hands on."

"Are you sure? I mean, we're about to enter the Twilight Zone."

"No need to get all geeky about it. I'm in. I have to be."

"Why's that?"

Spud's head droops and he stops walking. "See, I tell my counselor everything. Except for some reason I never mentioned the Rituals. And just then, when you were giving your little soliloquy, I finally worked out why." He sighs. "It's like, of all the stupid things I've done at Brookbank High, this is the only one I'm really ashamed of."

Without thinking about it, I give Spud an awkward man-hug, like professional athletes do knowing they shouldn't but—aw, shucks—they're just that happy. Spud stares at me like I just committed a cardinal sin, so I cough ostentatiously and get back to business.

"You got the Alternative Yearbook with you?" I ask, and Spud taps his bag affirmatively. "Okay, we're off to room 225."

Spud grabs my shoulder. "Room 225? Isn't that where GRRLS meets?"

"Yep. But they usually meet during English period."

"Oh, yeah. I forgot about that." He visibly relaxes.

"Except for today."

"When are they meeting today?"

I study my watch like it matters. "Let's see... Right about now."

35

The closer we get to room 225, the slower Spud walks. By the time we're passing 224, he's practically immobile.

"Come on, Spud. It's going to be fine."

"Are you sure?"

"Absolutely," I lie.

"Um, okay."

We nudge forward a few more feet until we're looking through the window in the door of room 225. Morgan is sitting on the teacher's desk, chairing the emergency session of GRRLS. I hope that she'll be the one to see me, but no such luck. Instead, Kayla catches a glimpse of me, and within seconds the classroom is rattling with boos. Morgan turns around, gives a curt nod, and then I pull Spud away.

"I thought you said it'd be fine?"

"They weren't booing you," I say comfortingly.

"They're going to lynch us."

"Probably."

"Geez, Kev. Like, why don't we just go back and take our chances with Brandon?"

"We still might." I drag Spud along the corridor and down the main staircase. "Listen, Spud, do you trust me?"

"No, of course not. Why the hell would I trust you?"

"So what was all that stuff about my speech changing your life?"

"It doesn't mean I trust you."

"Great!"

At the bottom of the staircase, I hesitate by the double doors leading to the Quad. I have serious misgivings about this part of the plan, but Spud seems to be reading my thoughts—he mumbles something about his counselor and then clomps onto the thick lush grass, while I follow close behind. Then he turns around expectantly, and I point to the doors. Almost immediately the entire contingent of GRRLS comes pouring through, all death stares and hands on hips and concentrated estrogen.

"Um, hello," I say, once they've fallen into silence. "So you're probably wondering why Morgan told you to come down here, huh?"

Actually, they just look like they're waiting for a chance to pummel me, but I pretend they've answered in the affirmative as it makes it easier for me to continue.

"Yeah, so the reason you're here is that—"

"I'm really sorry," babbles Spud, like they've just threatened him with thumbscrews. "I wholeheartedly apologize for any part I have played in the offensive endeavors of the so-called Graduation Rituals."

There's a lengthy silence as they process this impressive oratory display, then they're all staring at me again. But it's clear that Spud has softened their resistance, and as I resume my speech I'm not so afraid that this will be my last day on earth. I even catch Abby smiling at me reassuringly, which really helps.

"Yeah, so I ... oh, the hell with it," I shout, pulling the book from my bag. "This is the Book of Busts. I'm sorry I ever made you care about something as meaningless as this. And since the information in it belongs to no one but you, I hereby return it to you, to do with as you please." I throw it on the grass with a flourish.

"And this is the Alternative Yearbook," adds Spud, "which ... well, actually, I never got around to filling it in, but if I had it would have been pretty offensive as well, and I'm sorry for that." He throws it on top of the Book of Busts.

"And now," says Morgan solemnly, stepping forward to join us, "I think it's time to free ourselves from the influence of bad literature forever."

Everyone holds their breath as she pulls a bottle of perfume and a lighter from her purse. She douses the open leather-bound books with Calvin Klein Euphoria, then flicks her lighter. Instantly the worn pages are devoured by flames, and the air fills with smoke and cheering.

Abby points to a row of windows running along one side of the Quad. Behind them, the remaining proponents of the Graduation Rituals are staring at us with seething hatred.

Without hesitation, Morgan takes charge. "Sisters," she cries, "I want you to make a note of each of those boys. Whatever happens, they won't have a dance at the prom. Agreed?"

Suddenly everyone is cheering again, and Zach comes out to investigate. The sight of Taylor applauding wildly probably didn't sit too well with him. He ought to realize he's vastly outnumbered, but he doesn't seem to have a firm grasp on the situation, so he strides forward until he's surrounded by GRRLS.

"What are you doing here, Taylor?" he asks with a bemused expression. "You're not a dyke."

Taylor just shakes her head. "Isn't it time you crawled back to your cave and played some more drinking games?"

"Screw you, bitch."

There's an eerie silence. Taylor looks like she can't decide whether to laugh or scream or punch Zach.

Spud steps forward. "I think you need to leave, Zach," he says calmly.

Zach blinks in surprise, then regains his composure. "Oh yeah? Why?"

"Because I'm feeling really tense." Suddenly, Spud is doing a passable impression of Bruce Banner just before he becomes the Hulk. "And I don't think I can be held responsible for what I might do."

Zach's eyes narrow, and in a rare moment of intellectual clarity he takes a step back. "Yeah, well ... fine."

Zach hasn't made it back through the double doors before everyone is laughing and cheering again. All except Taylor, who plants a kiss on Spud's cheek.

"My knight in shining armor," she bubbles.

Spud blushes.

"Oh, the fire's gone out already," says Jessica, directing everyone's attention to the sad pile of charred sheets on the ground. She proposes a moment of silence.

Morgan leans in toward me and whispers, "I'd have to say that went pretty well."

"Yeah, it actually did."

"You did a brave thing, Kevin. Everyone here knows that now. I'm proud of you. You should be proud of yourself too."

I look around and see that Abby is smiling, and suddenly everything seems worthwhile. And I really do feel proud.

"Ah, wonderful," cackles Principal Jefferies, appearing beside the double doors. "A bumper crop! So many punishments, so little time!"

36

No one says a word, but the air continues to hum. I look around and realize the excitement our activities have generated. Faces are glued to every window, watching as Jefferies steps out onto the Quad. They know they're watching the high-school equivalent of a train wreck, and no one wants to miss a thing.

Zach is conspicuously absent, and the other members of Brandon's posse have left their places behind the windows. Given his infatuation with the baseball team, Jefferies probably waited for them to make themselves scarce before pouncing.

"Well now," he booms, trying to pretend that he's not enjoying this immensely, "who do we have here? Spud Beasley, naturally, and ... Kevin Mopsely! Hmmm, didn't expect to see you out here, Mr. Mopsely. And on to the female contingent—"

"We're GRRLS," interjects Abby, preempting the tedious process of identifying everyone by name.

"I can see that."

"No, *GRRLS*," says Morgan. She draws out the word as if it had three syllables and no vowels.

"What?"

"GRRLS—the Women's Studies group taught by Dr. Donaldson."

"Oh. Well, that's nice, I suppose. You'll all be able to arrange a little meeting for your club this Friday evening, instead of attending prom."

"What?" shrieks Taylor. "But that's not fair!"

"Oh, but I assure you it is, Miss Carson. In fact, it's supremely generous of me to give you such a mild punishment, all things considered."

Taylor looks like she's ready to burst, but Morgan steps forward, a model of calm. She has a presence I've never noticed before.

"We understand your position, of course," she says.

"Good."

"However, I should remind you that three weeks ago you permitted the male participants of the Graduation Rituals to hold a similarly sized meeting on this very spot, and we demand nothing more than equal treatment."

"And need I remind *you*, Miss Giddes," sneers Jefferies, "that the boys you're talking about didn't set fire to the Quad."

"Oh." Morgan looks over at me for help, but all I can do is shrug; he's got us there. She takes a deep breath. "Well, never mind, we won't need to meet on Friday because we already have a meeting planned for Thursday evening ... while the baseball final's being played."

Jefferies seems to have trouble making the connection, but then he gasps. "B-But you ... you're practically the whole cheerleading squad. You have to attend the game. It's your *duty* to cheer our boys on."

Morgan sighs and wrings her hands. "What a pity. Such terrible timing, but the meeting absolutely can't be moved."

"But you're the *cheerleaders*. It would be an embarrassment to the school if you weren't there."

"Such a shame," agrees Morgan.

"Well, if you don't attend this game, you can forget about making the squad next year!" he quips with an evil leer.

"We're seniors."

The standoff between Morgan and Jefferies is all the more compelling because it's being viewed by almost half the school now, some of them hanging out of open windows to hear better. Spud glances at me and raises his eyebrows. I raise mine back.

"Now listen here, Miss Giddes. I will not be blackmailed into renegotiating your punishment."

"Of course not," says Morgan, like the very implication offends her. "Can we go now, please?"

"But ... I'm not finished. I mean, couldn't you reschedule your meeting? It's really important that we have a convincing display of Brookbank High spirit."

"I see that," agrees Morgan. "After all, it will look awful when all those TV cameras show that the cheerleading squad isn't even there. And when they find out that we've all been banned from our own senior prom … well, just think of the negative publicity. I'd be surprised if anyone joined the cheerleading squad ever again."

It's clear that she's won. Now it's just a matter of how long Jefferies holds out before capitulating.

"Hmmm," he murmurs, shuffling his feet. "On further consideration, I'm thinking it may be advantageous if the cheerleaders are able to attend prom."

"And everyone else too, of course," she says amiably.

"Absolutely not."

"Oh dear. I suppose we'll be holding our meeting as planned, then."

Jefferies looks ready to explode. "Fine! Everybody present is entitled to attend prom."

"That would be nice." Morgan seems like she doesn't much care either way.

"In return, however, I expect the full cheerleading squad to attend the game on Thursday. Is that clear?"

"Yes," says Morgan, a little too readily.

"The *baseball* game," he clarifies.

"Yes."

"And you'll wear your Brookbank High cheerleading outfits."

"Yes."

"And I expect to hear you cheering."

"Yes."

"Loudly."

"Yes."

"Hmmm." Jefferies has clearly run out of legal fine print, so he huffs a couple of times and turns to leave.

I notice that Ms. Kowalski is hovering in the doorway, and I wonder how much of the spectacle she's witnessed.

"So if we do all of the things you just said, we can attend prom, right?" Morgan asks just as he reaches the double doors. "We have your word on that?" She sweeps her hand through 360 degrees to indicate that there are a few hundred witnesses.

He looks around, becoming aware for the first time just how many students have been eavesdropping on the Quad performance. "Yes, Ms. Giddes," he snaps. "You have my word."

Everybody screams and cheers and hugs all at once. All except Morgan, who smiles like she finds the whole thing incredibly amusing.

37

"Won't it bug you at all to see GRRLS cheering on the group they've sworn to bring down?" I ask Abby as we approach the bleachers.

She doesn't say a word, just smiles enigmatically.

We're arriving late so we won't have to sit through too much of the game, but Abby actually seems quite excited to be here. As we round the edge of the bleachers, I look up and see that the score is already 5-1. Oh well, no surprise there.

"Pretty shocking, huh?" says Abby, pointing at the scoreboard.

I look again and realize that we're *down* 5-1. Okay, that's shocking. And fantastic.

Brookbank is fielding, and they're arguing with one another, spewing obscenities like they're codes for defensive plays. Brandon flips Ryan the bird, and Ryan reciprocates, and I have a warm and fuzzy feeling about what I'm witnessing.

The opposing batter steps up and drives a routine ground ball straight at Brandon. He bends down and ... bobbles it, and suddenly another runner has scored: 6-1.

A cheer erupts in deafening stereo and I look down toward the dugouts, where the opposition cheerleaders have been joined by Brookbank's own. Beside me, Abby laughs and gives her friends an appreciative whoop.

"What?" she says, as she senses me staring at her. "You didn't really think they'd cheer for *our* team, did you?"

"But what about the stuff Jefferies said?"

"Fine print's a bitch, ain't it? He told them they had to attend this game, wear the Brookbank outfits, and cheer loudly. I'd say they're doing all of those things. Wouldn't you?"

It's pure genius. All of the cheerleaders sport ear-to-ear grins as they applaud each miscue by Brookbank's team, and Jefferies has the good sense to stay out of their way as long as the TV cameras are rolling. Even Paige looks flushed with excitement—she edges her way to the front of the group and performs a sexy belly dance for the camera long after everyone else has stopped cheering.

I glance down at the Brookbank dugout and see Spud. I figure he can't be impressed by Ryan's pitching tonight, but then he looks over his shoulder and winks at me. Although this is his team, I think he's secretly thrilled to see what's happening. While he's distracted, Taylor dashes over and gives him a quick kiss. Zach notices and yells an obscenity from first base that's caught on camera, so Jefferies demands that the coach take him out of the game. Then Brandon mouths off at the coach for removing Zach, so he gets benched as well.

It's still only the fourth inning, but for the first time

in my life I'll willingly stay until the end of the game. I wouldn't miss this for anything.

Brookbank loses 13-2.

Morgan insists that we join the cheerleaders at IHOP, so Abby and I crush together on the passenger seat of Morgan's Miata. I have a boner almost the whole way, but Abby either doesn't notice or prefers to ignore it. Can't say I blame her, really.

At IHOP, eight of us cram into a four-person booth. There's a lot of girl-bonding stuff going on, but girl-bonding stuff is kind of hot, so I don't mind being sandwiched in the middle of it all.

It's not clear if anyone really wants to eat, but a waitress appears expectantly beside the booth and immediately stares at me. For a moment I'm confused, but then it all comes flooding back.

"Um, hello, Keira," I say.

Now everyone's looking at me weirdly, and I can't even make a hasty exit to the men's room because I'm squeezed in. Keira remains silent. I have a bad feeling about this.

"So Keira," I gulp, "I'm really sorry about what happened the last time I was here—"

Keira shakes her head. "S'okay. You don't need to apologize. I know you tried not to order anything. I really appreciated it."

"Anyone else wondering what's going on here?" Taylor asks.

Keira sighs. "Oh, a while back this guy came in with my ex, Ryan. And Ryan made me buy food for him and his friends. And they ordered a ton of stuff. All except this guy." She nods in my direction.

"Aw, Kevin really is Brookbank's very own Renaissance man," declares Morgan, which sounds especially good when there are six other girls to hear her say it.

We've barely finished placing our order when Keira glances toward the door and steps back skittishly. She thrusts her order pad into the pocket of her apron and rushes off toward the kitchen.

"What was all that ab—" begins Kayla, but then Brandon and the rest of the baseball team are standing in Keira's place.

"Hello, Mopsely," spits Brandon.

For a few seconds he simply stands there, shifting his weight from foot to foot. I'm trying to think of something to say when suddenly he sprawls across the table, grabs my T-shirt, and punches me in the nose. It hurts like hell.

Abby jumps up. "Get away from him, Brandon."

"Oh yeah, I forgot... You're his ugly bitch, right?"

I wait for Abby to hit him, but she doesn't. She just laughs. "Um, let me get this straight... You just lost the city championship, and your own cheerleaders chose to support the opposition, but you still reckon you have the right to call me an 'ugly bitch'? Don't you realize that right now you're the biggest loser in school history? And that's a truly monumental achievement. So pardon me if I say that being called a bitch by you doesn't exactly mean too much."

Brandon's gearing up for another insult when Keira reemerges with the rest of the wait staff and a few knife-wielding chefs.

"That's him," she says, pointing at Ryan. "That's the guy who made me give him free stuff. And he...he never even liked me that much," she sniffles.

An elderly guy steps forward and prods Ryan in the chest. "Son, you and your buddies best get the hell out of my restaurant. And don't never come back, you hear me?"

"Or what?" snorts Brandon.

"Or I guarantee that everything you order will contain a few extra magic ingredients you never even asked for."

Ryan's already edging toward the door. Reluctantly, the rest of the team joins him.

"So long, losers," shouts Brandon.

We watch him leave and then erupt in laughter.

"Your nose is bleeding, Kev," says Abby, looking concerned.

Taylor takes a peek. "Oh, I've got something to stop that." She rummages around in her bag and pulls out a white cotton plug. "Just stay still."

There's total silence as Taylor leans toward me and delicately pushes the plug up my nose. Then everyone relaxes again, giggling once more about Brandon's recent proclamations.

And even though everyone's staring at me, I laugh too, because Brandon really is the stupidest person I've ever met.

38

I guess you're going to say 'I told you so,' huh?"

"Hardly seems necessary," Abby replies matter-of-factly.

We're walking home together. It's a couple of miles, but it's a mild evening and I'm on a high.

"It's just that ... he could be cool. And he made me feel like I wasn't a geek. He can be a nice guy, you know."

Abby just shakes her head. "Your dad can be a nice guy, Kevin. Doesn't excuse what he's done."

"I guess not." I smile at her, but she's looking away. "Well, I'm glad everything's back to normal now."

"You're kidding, right? You really think everything's back to normal?"

"Isn't it?"

"No, Kev," she whispers, "it's not. What about the pop group?"

Oh yeah. I forgot about that.

"You left us and you never even had the guts to say so," she continues. "You're the best performer this school has known and you turned your back on music. But even worse, you turned your back on me. You're my best friend and you treated me like crap."

"I'm really sorry, Abby. At least I've apologized to everyone now—"

"But I'm not *everyone*." She stops walking and stares at me like she's trying to explain a really easy math problem. "In case you've forgotten, I didn't hook up with you to inflate my measurements, or to get back at some other guy. I did it because I love you, and I thought you liked me too."

"I know. I'm sorry."

She looks hurt. "You're sorry that I love you?"

"No, I'm sorry for everything that's happened. You know, for the things I did."

"The *things* you did?"

"Yeah. For all of it."

"All of it?" She shakes her head, stares at the ground. "That's the best you can do?"

"What do you want me to say, Abby?"

"I want you to say you're sorry—not about *all of it*, but about *me*, and what you did to me. And I want you to say it like you mean it. And I want…"

I give her a few seconds, but she's silent and still. "What do you want?"

She peers up and sighs wearily. "Listen, Kev. I always dreamed high school would end with you walking next door to escort me to prom. I even thought it was a sure thing. But I waited and waited for you to ask me. And then, last week,

I bought myself a ticket. Because whatever else you've done to me, I'm not going to let you spoil prom as well."

I nod, but I'm not exactly sure what she wants me to say, so we walk the rest of the way in silence. When we reach her house, she heads up the front walk without saying good-bye.

"I'm sorry, Abby." I say suddenly. "I'm really, really sorry. I mean it."

She turns and smiles, but it's a distant smile. "Then prove it, Kevin. Show me you're still the same as ever, 'cause I'm done talking. Words are cheap, as they say." She strides away and pulls her front door open roughly. She doesn't look back.

I wait a few seconds, then take a deep breath and trudge one door down. I'm barely indoors when I almost trip over Mom—she's on her knees tickling Matt the Mutt's belly.

"Hello," she says.

"Hey," I mumble.

And there the conversation ends, just as it has every day this week. I'm about to slide on by when I remember Abby's words: "But I'm not *everyone*." Mom's still petting the dog, but her movements seem deliberate and tense, like she wants to say something but doesn't know how. We're at a stalemate, and I know that since it's my fault we're in this situation, it's also my responsibility to make things better.

"Morgan says they all wish they hadn't asked you to leave," I say, breaking the ice.

She doesn't look up, but I can see she's smiling. "That's all right. Tell her it's sweet of her to say so."

More silence.

I take a deep breath. "Look, Mom, I'm sorry. I screwed up, I know I did . . . and I know I hurt you." Mom nods but doesn't say anything. "And you were right, talking to Dad did help. Just maybe not the way you thought it would."

"I suspect it helped *exactly* the way I thought it would. Don't forget, I know your father better than you do, Kevin." Mom's crying now, but she's still smiling too, so I don't think she's angry or sad. "And although I couldn't bear to think of you following in his footsteps—not after everything that's happened—I had to give you the chance."

"What do you mean?"

"I mean . . . given his recent e-mails, I had a good idea what he'd say to you." She puffs out her cheeks. "And either you'd like what you heard and stay with him, or you wouldn't. And then you came back."

"But he wasn't always like this, right? This isn't who he really is."

Mom wipes the tears away with the back of her hand and studies the floor. "Actually, honey, it is."

"What?"

"His affair with Kimberly wasn't the first, and it probably won't be the last. I knew what he was like before we got married, but . . . oh, I flattered myself that he'd change for me. Like I was that special, you know?" She laughs ruefully, then shakes her head. "Well, I was wrong. Over time he got bored of me. I guess he wanted something else, something more . . . who really knows? Maybe being with Kimberly made him feel special somehow, but I doubt he loved her. I don't think he'll ever understand that when you find the right person, you don't need other people to reassure you that you're special. Because it's enough to hear it from the person who means it the most."

Mom makes eye contact for the first time. I settle down on the floor beside her because I need to keep talking.

"I totally blew it with Abby. She was there for me all along, and I just—"

"You let her down, honey, but you didn't blow it."

"Same difference."

"No, it's not. I still love your father even though he doesn't love me. Despite everything he's done, I love him. And believe me, there are times I hate myself for it too. But you know what they say: even when the flames disappear, the embers keep burning."

I think of the family portraits at the top of the stairs— how many days, months, years will pass before she can finally bring herself to take Dad's down? And how many days, months, years before Dad decides to put up a photo of any of us in his apartment? Mom can't let our family go; Dad won't acknowledge we ever existed. They're on opposite sides of an impossible divide. Surely that's not true of Abby and me?

"I don't know," I say, thinking out loud. "Some of the things she said—"

"She's angry and hurt, and no wonder. So now you need to be patient. Give her time to realize you're still the same person she'd grown to love. It's the least you can do." And Mom's right about that.

I lean over and stroke the dog gently, and for the first time in weeks he doesn't growl at me. In fact, he nuzzles my hand before falling asleep against my leg.

"It's nice to talk again," I say.

"Yes, it is."

Mom kisses my cheek like I'm five years old, which I take as a sign of forgiveness and as a cue to escape. I'm almost at the stairs when she coughs delicately, stopping me in my tracks.

"Kevin, honey, I hate to ask, but … there's one thing that still bothers me."

I gulp. "Um, what is it?"

She bites a fingernail and narrows her eyes.

"Why are you wearing a tampon up your nose?"

39

I figure that everyone except me will be fashionably late to prom, but when I arrive there's already a crowd waiting to get inside. Immediately in front of me, GRRLS forms a snaking line of slinky dresses—without a single tuxedo to spoil the effect. The few couples who somehow missed or ignored Brookbank's feminist revolution are so heavily out-numbered that they look embarrassed to be here. It must be the first major event in school history where the partnerless dorks feel cooler than the hip, beautiful couples. I appreci-ate this change—it benefits people like me.

The line is moving slowly and eventually stops alto-gether. I hear raised voices ahead of me, so I pull away to have a peek. Morgan and Taylor are standing side by side, holding their ground as Jefferies shakes his head, staring defiantly at a point slightly above their heads.

"But we did what you asked," Morgan insists.

"You did no such thing. You were an embarrassment to the school and everything it stands for."

"No, the baseball team is the embarrassment," Taylor corrects him. "We were simply standing up for ourselves."

"Turn around and go home, girls. And be grateful that your punishment ends here."

"This is completely ... " begins Morgan, but then trails off.

Ms. Kowalski emerges from inside and sidles up to Jefferies, holding a finger to her lips. He spins around.

"Oh hello, Jane. I was just telling these girls that—"

"They should hurry up and come inside." Ms. K smiles innocently. "I wondered what had been holding up the line."

"B-But the game last night," he stammers.

"Yes. They came, they dressed, they cheered."

"But they cheered for the wrong team!"

"Well, you didn't tell them which team to cheer for, did you, Carl? And you're always telling me how important it is to be specific with one's instructions."

Jefferies is livid, but Ms. K is already ushering GRRLS inside to avoid further incident. They trail along behind Morgan, their unofficial leader, all smirks and giggles. And suddenly I'm at the front of the line.

"Hold on, Mr. Mopsely," sneers Jefferies. "What a coincidence to find you standing beside the cheerleaders again. Weren't you one of the participants in their Quad stunt?"

"Well, I wouldn't call myself a *participant*, exactly."

"Then what would you call yourself?"

"Um ... a bystander?"

"Oh really? Rumor has it you provided them with the Book of Busts. Is that true?"

Ms. K stops in her tracks and peers over her shoulder; I imagine that hearing Jefferies refer to the Book of Busts has not improved her mood. As our eyes meet I can tell that we're both considering the current status of our cold war, so I try to convey through telepathy that I'm sorry for everything I've done and would like to declare a truce. Somehow, Ms. K seems to understand.

"Carl, I'm sure you're about to congratulate Kevin on bringing an end to that galling tradition, but in the interest of time, how about we just let him in immediately, instead?"

"But Jane, I—"

"Carl," sighs Ms. K, "let's just move things along here, okay? At the rate we're going, some of the students won't even make it to prom."

It's about the most assertive thing I've ever heard her say, and Jefferies looks distinctly hot under the collar. With a flick of her head, Ms. Kowalski indicates that I should jog inside while he seems too distracted to stop me. No wonder she's my favorite teacher.

The school gym is decked out with streamers, balloons, and banners sporting French place names. A model Eiffel Tower that was a prop in the last school musical stands proudly in the middle of the floor. I sense a theme here, but I've always studiously avoided anyone associated with prom organization, so I can't say for sure whether it's deliberate.

At the front of the gym, on a flimsily constructed stage, a string trio massacres a Mozart Divertimento. It's an excruciating experience, and midway through their performance someone steps forward and asks them to wrap it up. As if aware of their own ineptitude they don't even bother to finish the piece properly, so the music sort of fizzles out. In a pauper's grave somewhere in Vienna, Mozart is thanking them for stopping.

"Geez, that was seriously hideous," says Kayla, shaking her head like she still can't understand why she was made to hear it.

"Yeah, it really was."

Silence.

"Listen, Kayla, I just want to say I'm sorry I put you through ... you know ... that stuff. And the date."

Kayla waves it off. "You've already apologized."

"Yeah, but not to you personally. And Abby made me realize that I owe you a personal apology."

"Yeah, you really screwed things up with her, huh? I mean, if I'd known she was into you I'd never have gone on that so-called date. I still find it pretty incredible that someone as cool as her is interested in you. No offense."

"No offense taken," I assure her. And I'm really not offended, because she's right—Abby is way cooler than me, and it's a miracle that she ever wanted to date me.

Right on cue, Abby, Nathan, and Caitlin take the stage, launching into one of our jazz arrangements. The sound is so much better than the string trio that everyone is immediately into the music, dancing or nodding their heads rhythmically, even though they'd never be caught dead listening to music like this outside of prom.

GRRLS leads the way, performing a raunchy, hip-grind-ing series of moves that has every guy staring with an open mouth. But Morgan and her sisters don't even seem to notice. It's like they've somehow moved beyond the need for boys completely, which would be depressing if they didn't look so utterly contented.

By the third song, a couple of dorky chess-playing seniors with acne summon the courage to approach Morgan and her friends and ask for a dance. It's the most improbable request in history, but GRRLS welcomes them into the throng, passing the boys along the line until they've danced with every girl. Straightaway, all the geeks, dorks, stoners, and losers gravitate into the GRRLS vortex and surrender themselves to the irresistible allure of Morgan and company.

The only geek who remains apart is me, because I'm busy focusing on the quartet. More accurately, I'm focusing on Abby, watching as her hair whips across the front of the double bass. She's dyed it so that thick red streaks punctuate her natural brunette, and her red satin dress matches the streaks. But more than anything I notice how completely unself-conscious she is as she lets herself go with the music. It makes her look amazingly confident and sexy. I get the feeling a few of the other guys are checking her out too.

Nathan strikes up the first of the classic pop songs, and again everyone gives in to the urge to dance. For a while I join them, but then I stop so I can listen to the music properly, enjoying the precision of the ensemble and the energy of the performance. How did I ever turn my back on this?

The song ends and I initiate the applause, striding to the edge of the stage and screaming my appreciation. And even though I wish I could be up there with them, right now I just want them to know how good they sound. Nathan and Caitlin laugh as they see me, jumping up and down and whooping until I'm red in the face. But Abby doesn't smile. She just stares me down until the applause dies out, by which time everyone is watching our interaction with morbid fascination.

I feel frozen to the spot as Abby gently lowers her double bass and approaches the front of the stage, her hands clasped firmly behind her back. When she's almost directly in front of me, she bends down and raises her right hand menacingly. I close my eyes and brace myself.

Suddenly I feel the palm of her hand on the back of my head, and her lips against mine. I open my eyes. We're kissing. We're really kissing. Behind me, everyone cheers.

"Welcome back, you dork," Abby murmurs, her breath like a gentle summer breeze.

Straight away, Nathan launches into the opening bars of "California Dreamin'." Abby is biting her lip and smiling, and I can't resist the urge to kiss her again. But then she pulls away and brings her other hand around so that I can see it.

Grasped between her fingers is my flute, already pieced together and ready to play.

For a couple of seconds I'm too stunned to react, but then I leap onto the stage and take the flute from her.

A moment later I begin singing and playing the arrangement she wrote for me from memory.

40

For better or worse, I don't feel self-conscious standing in front of my peers, warbling my way through a song that most of them have only ever heard their grandparents play. All that matters is that Abby has forgiven me, so I throw everything I've got into the performance.

The song ends and the audience erupts. I can see the DJ standing just offstage, waiting to take over, but the crowd screams for an encore. We run through the entire pop song set again, and this time I join in with each one.

A month ago I was afraid that people would think we were total losers for playing this stuff, but now I see that we're the nearest thing Brookbank has to a bona fide pop group; this must be the kind of high that keeps the Rolling Stones performing, even though they're almost two hundred years old.

In the middle of the gym, GRRLS is no longer a unified

group—most of them have split and partnered with boys. To an outsider, our senior class would look like the most perfectly functional collection of eighteen-year-olds imaginable. The past has been forgotten—everyone prefers the look of the present.

We end the set with a reprise of "California Dreamin'," and this time I stand between Abby and Caitlin, leaning from side to side in time with them. It's not exactly original, and it's certainly not sexy, but it feels surprisingly cool.

And then Brandon and his cronies walk in.

We manage to keep going for almost the whole song, but they're wreaking havoc on some of the more skittish couples, pushing the boys aside and sliding in for an intimate grind with the poor unsuspecting girls. Eventually we look at one another and bring the music to a premature close.

Brandon looks up, surprised. "Don't stop for us," he shouts. "Even crap music is better than no music."

The DJ spies his opportunity and jumps in with a hip-hop cover of "Twist and Shout." Brandon laughs triumphantly and returns his attention to separating the couples around him.

"Come on," says Abby. "We're going down there."

"Can't we just stay on the stage?" I ask hopefully.

"Don't be a wuss, Kev. If I wasn't going to let you ruin my senior prom, I'm sure as hell not going to let Brandon Trent do it."

Caitlin and Nathan and I tag along behind Abby as she jumps off the stage and joins the throngs cavorting in mini-circles throughout the gym. Just ahead of us, Zach is making a beeline for Taylor, who has her arms wrapped around Spud's broad shoulders.

"Hey, Taylor," Zach screams above the music. "What the hell are you doing?"

Taylor doesn't hesitate. "I'm dancing with my boyfriend."

"You've got to be kidding me. Spud's a retard. Spud's a—"

With a lightning-fast thrust of his arm, Spud sends Zach sprawling across the floor. Zach stays down for a few seconds, then struggles to his feet. He clasps both hands tightly over his mouth, apparently unaware that his nose is bleeding quite impressively.

"My tooth," he whimpers. "You chipped my tooth!" Blood from his nose runs over his fingers as he scampers away.

I turn to Taylor. "Looks to me like he might need one of your tampons."

Taylor blushes. "Oh, you worked out what that was, huh?"

"My mom told me."

Taylor and Abby laugh, and even though I should feel embarrassed, I somehow don't.

Morgan joins us and gives Abby a hug. "What's so funny?"

Taylor laughs again. "Oh, Kevin was just saying that—"

"He likes the DJ," Abby interrupts, trying to spare me further humiliation. I give her a kiss.

"Ready to go to third now, Morgan?" drawls Brandon, stumbling toward us and pushing Abby out of the way.

"As I recall, we never got past first, Brandon, and that's

not about to change." Morgan turns up her nose as if he smells; which, come to think of it, he does—the odor of cheap booze hangs about him whenever he opens his mouth. I guess he decided to try out his fake ID.

"You're really tight, but I guess all virgins are like that," slurs Brandon, groping her butt.

Morgan pushes him away. "Get off me, you jerk."

"I'll do whatever the hell I want," he grunts, pulling her toward him and forcing his lips onto hers.

Morgan slaps at Brandon's face frantically, while Abby pummels him with an impressive barrage of right and left hooks, but nothing slows him down. After a couple seconds, he swats Abby away like she's nothing more than an irritating insect. As I see her look of outrage and glimpse Morgan's utter horror, something inside me snaps. I grab hold of Brandon's tuxedo jacket and pull him away, then hurl him across the floor with every ounce of strength I can muster. He's off-balance, drunk, and completely unable to regain his footing before he crashes headfirst into the model Eiffel tower, which collapses on top of him.

It feels as if everyone is waiting to exhale. I know that any second now Brandon will get up and beat the crap out of me; it seems likes the natural, inevitable conclusion to this episode of my life.

But instead, with typically impeccable timing, Jefferies approaches our group. He's incensed that the backdrop for the prom photos is lying in a heap in the middle of the floor. Ms. K appears too, and kneels down beside Brandon's prone figure.

"What just happened here?" Jefferies bellows.

I look around the group. Abby grasps my hand as Morgan blinks back tears and steps forward. I can tell she doesn't want to have to say out loud what just happened, but she won't allow me to take the fall, either.

She coughs. "Brandon was—"

"Drunk!" shrieks Ms. K. "Carl, just smell this boy's breath. He clearly passed out and fell into the tower." She jams her hands onto her hips. "It seems that every year some students feel the need to flaunt the rules. Well, I trust you'll be dealing with him most harshly."

"I-I certainly will," Jefferies assures her.

Together they disentangle Brandon's body from the mess of papier-mâché girders. As they carry him out of the hall, I notice the rest of his posse stumbling uneasily toward the exits. Nobody tries to stop them.

Morgan coughs again. "Thank you, Kevin. That was very chivalrous of you." She steps over and gives me a peck on the cheek.

"Hey," says Abby, pretending to be annoyed. "You want to kiss my boyfriend, you need to ask me for permission."

No one seems at all surprised to hear her call me her boyfriend, but I spin around and raise my eyebrows inquiringly.

"What?" She grins. "In the new spirit of sexual equality, I decided to take the initiative. Don't you want to be my boyfriend?"

"Actually, I'd like that very much."

Abby leans in and kisses me, and straight away we're full-on. It feels amazing—the perfect distraction from my brush with death moments before—but I still have something to say, and I need to say it now.

"I'm so sorry, Abby. I'm sorry for everything I said and did, and for all the ways I hurt you and took you for granted. I don't deserve you."

She half-smiles and nods approvingly. "Apology accepted. Now I think we should try to move on ... Kissing would be a good start." She leans forward expectantly.

Another kiss, more delicate this time. But something still doesn't feel right.

"I really mean it, Abby. I feel so guilty about everything."

Abby sighs and rolls her eyes. "Well, I think it's time you looked on the funny side. Now that your obsession with breasts is behind you, you have to admit that it was all kind of weird."

"Yeah, it was."

"And you certainly learned a lesson."

I can't help chuckling. "Yeah. I really got busted."

"Bust-what? ... Did you just say *bust?*"

"No, no, no." I take a deep breath. "I said busted."

"Oh. You mean you screwed up."

"Yeah. As your mom would say, I made a boo-boo."

"A boob-what? ... Did you just say *boob?*

"No!" I can feel my pulse quickening.

Abby narrows her eyes suspiciously. "Geez, Kev. I thought this was supposed to be an apology."

"It is. It really is. I just ... it's not coming out quite right, you know?"

"Well, I'm just glad you agree that you were kind of stupid."

"Absolutely, yeah. I've been a twit."

Her jaw drops open. "A tit? … Did you just say *tit*?"

Oh crap.

"God, no! I wouldn't say anything like that. I'm past all that stuff now. I'm … I'm … "

"You're what?"

"I'm … " I begin, but then I notice Abby's mouth twisting into a smile.

"Easily manipulated?" she suggests, biting her lower lip.

"What?"

"I'm just messing with you, Kev … But you *are* easily manipulated, you know."

Oh my God, she was kidding. I can't believe this.

"I am not easily manipulated," I say confidently, but Abby just laughs. "Not always … I mean, sometimes I—"

"Shut up and kiss me," she groans, and this time I'm happy to oblige—it seems safer than apologizing.

I hesitate just a moment, but then our mouths come together and we kiss.

Again.

And again.

I guess that being manipulated has its upside.

©2008 Audrey John

About the Author

Antony John was born in England and raised on a balanced diet of fish and chips, obscure British comedies, and ABBA's greatest hits. In a fit of teenage rebellion, he decided to pursue a career in classical music, culminating in a BA from Oxford University and a PhD from Duke University. Along the way, he worked as an ice cream seller on a freezing English beach, a tour guide in the Netherlands, a chauffeur in Switzerland, a barista in Seattle, and a university professor. Writing by night, he spends his days as a stay-at-home dad—the only job that allows him to wear his favorite pair of sweatpants all the time. He lives in St. Louis with his family. Visit Antony online at www.antonyjohn.net.

Acknowledgments

A debut novel rarely sees the light of day without having a fairly hefty support team, and *Busted* is no exception. Kevin Mopsely and I owe an impossibly deep debt of gratitude to Ted Malawer, my indefatigable agent—scholar, champion, and all-around nice guy—for making it all possible, and Nadia Cornier, for sage advice at every step. To Andrew Karre, my nurturing and insightful editor, for coming up with all the best ideas in the novel and allowing me to pass them off as my own, and the A-Team at Flux: Gavin Duffy for the (literally) jaw-dropping cover; Sandy Sullivan for taking my mess of words and tying it up with a nice pink bow; Steffani Sawyer for the elegant interior design; and Brian Farrey for his stalwart mentorship through the promotional side of publication.

My heartfelt appreciation to Nick Green, Simon Hay, and Robyn Reed—my intrepid early readers—who took me to task on everything from mistimed humor to misunderstood feminist ideology (sometimes both at once); Carolyn Moores and Jonathan Prentice, for administering generous doses of unsolicited praise at just the right moments; Julie Pottinger and Megan Atwood, for professional guidance that kept the project moving in the right direction; and Charles and Sandy Odom—my parents-in-law—for putting the whole clan up and looking after us while the final draft of this book was being completed.

I would also like to extend my sincerest thanks to the Seattle Public Library, especially the Northeast branch, for procuring whatever I needed, whenever I needed it, and for not getting steamed up every time my son ruined their displays; the staff at the Coffee Crew and Tully's Five Corners, Seattle, for fine coffee, friendly banter, and rent-free comfy chairs; John Hubbard and Jim Graham-Brown—the kind of high school English teachers legends are made of—for having faith in my writing, and more importantly, faith in me; and Roy and Angela John—my parents—for making my childhood (even my teenage years!) perpetually joyful. The older I get, the more I realize what a feat that was, and what a tremendous goal for me as a parent. If I do it half as well as you guys, I'll consider myself a roaring success.

And Audrey—last on the list but first in all things—for impacting each and every page. We both know I couldn't have done it without you, and it means so much to have shared every moment of the writing, editing, and publication process with you, my greatest advocate. Here's to many more years of our crazy, breathtaking ride.